Hidden

ALSO BY SOPHIE JORDAN

Firelight

Vanish

SOPHIE JORDAN

Hidden

A Firelight Novel

OXFORD
UNIVERSITY PRESS

OXFORD
UNIVERSITY PRESS

Great Clarendon Street, Oxford OX2 6DP

Oxford University Press is a department of the University of Oxford.
It furthers the University's objective of excellence in research, scholarship,
and education by publishing worldwide in

Oxford   New York

Auckland   Cape Town   Dar es Salaam   Hong Kong   Karachi
Kuala Lumpur   Madrid   Melbourne   Mexico City   Nairobi
New Delhi   Shanghai   Taipei   Toronto

With offices in

Argentina   Austria   Brazil   Chile   Czech Republic   France   Greece
Guatemala   Hungary   Italy   Japan   Poland   Portugal   Singapore
South Korea   Switzerland   Thailand   Turkey   Ukraine   Vietnam

Oxford is a registered trade mark of Oxford University Press
in the UK and in certain other countries

British Library Cataloguing in Publication Data

Data available

ISBN: 978-0-19-275657-2

1 3 5 7 9 10 8 6 4 2

Printed in Great Britain

Paper used in the production of this book is a natural,
recyclable product made from wood grown in sustainable forests.
The manufacturing process conforms to the environmental
regulations of the country of origin.

For you, faithful reader

My love for you is a journey.

Anonymous

CHAPTER ONE

The air traps hot inside my lungs as I hover outside the van, peering within, studying the shadowed depths, so reminiscent of another van not so long ago. This one is empty, but soon I'll occupy its space. Alone. My eyes start to burn from staring so hard at my soon-to-be prison and I blink swiftly. This is my choice, I remind myself.

'You don't have to do this,' Will says, holding my hand, his fingers brushing back and forth against the inside of my wrist, making my pulse jump to life, and I suddenly remember how to breathe. With him, every-thing is always easier. Bearable.

Even this.

I nod even though fear twists like a hot poker inside me.

It takes everything I have to slip my hand free from his and grip the edge of the door. 'Yes. I do.'

'We can come up with another way—'

'No. This will work.' It's my idea. Of course I believe in it. I persuaded them all, countering their protests until they agreed. Will. Cassian. Tamra. We've already come this far. Left my sister several miles back, waiting, hidden away until Will and Cassian return for her.

Will's expression tightens, making him look older, tired. But still achingly beautiful. I blink and smooth my fingers against his face, along his square, bristly jaw. 'It's going to be all right,' I reassure him. 'Just stick with the plan.'

'Don't do anything stupid in there . . . don't try to be a hero—'

I press my fingers to his lips to silence him, and relish the firm, cool texture. His eyes soften, the gold, browns, and greens like a forest in fall. Something unfurls in my chest as it always does when he looks at me that way.

Drawing in a deep breath, I look over at Cassian, self-conscious that he's watching us. But he's staring out at the tree line, one shoe kicking the ground. Even so, I can feel him through our shared awareness of each other. He's trying hard to give Will and me our space, but I sense his active concentration to avoid looking at us . . . his struggle to hide the annoyance snaking through him.

I wait for him to glance over. Maybe I even will him to do so. I don't know. This whole we-share-a-bond thing is still new. When he finally looks, I nod at him. He gives a slight nod back.

I twirl a finger in a small circle and say loud enough that it's clear I'm addressing them both, 'Now turn around.'

The barest smile lifts Will's mouth, but he obliges. So does Cassian. With their backs to me, I strip, focusing on my movements, each one so deliberate—untying my shoes, stepping out of my jeans. I fold the clothes neatly into a pile, taking extra care . . . as if this action is of the utmost importance. I guess I'm stalling.

Naked, I stand and stare at Will's back. The smooth, grey cotton stretched taut over his strong shoulder blades. Air slides over me and the sun kisses my flesh. This is when I'm supposed to climb into the van and close the doors. This is when we head into the lion's den. Where they will leave me. Abandon me—at my request. If things go wrong . . . I give myself a mental shake. *Not going there.*

My throat tightens anyway. Suddenly modesty doesn't matter so much. I grasp Will's shoulder and force him around, plastering my lips to his in a kiss that feels a lot like goodbye. I give it everything. I put the memory of us into it. All we've been through. Our time in Chaparral. His family—*hunters*—trying to destroy me. Losing Miram. Corbin trying to kill him . . .

His hands wrap around my back. I kiss him until the familiar burn starts at my core and crawls up my windpipe. Face flushed hot, I break away, panting, yearning.

And naked.

Will's gaze flickers down, missing nothing before looking back up. His chest lifts high on an inhale. My cheeks burn hotter, but I still linger. Searing emotion flashes in his hazel eyes and I know I have to go. I have to go or I never will.

I jump in the van and start to pull the doors shut.

His voice stops me. 'Wait.'

I peer out at him.

'You have to manifest.' He holds up the ties.

'Oh.' How did I forget? We have to do this right. Bait the hook.

I step down. Standing there, I force the change. With my emotions high, body flushed and tingly in reaction to Will, it doesn't take long. I manifest quickly, my skin snapping tight, my wings pushing free with a faint crackle on the air.

Will gazes at me a moment, his admiration evident. It winds through me, melts me inside to see that he still can look at me, in my draki form, appreciatively. Just like he did the first time he saw me. Like I'm something beautiful, and not the creature his family hunts. It's a helpful boost to my confidence as I'm about to face the hazy bogeymen of my childhood—the enkros—the ones who send the hunters after my kind. At last their faces will be revealed to me. A tight, shuddery breath ripples through me.

Will quickly but gently ties my wrists, and then my wings. He avoids my eyes as he works, as though he can't bear to do this to me.

I feel the change come over Cassian as he turns. Doubt radiates from him as I'm bound like a captive before his very eyes.

Will looks up at my face as he helps me back into the van. I offer a smile. It feels weak, and forced, so I let the smile slip away and just communicate with my eyes. *This is right.*

Then I turn, positioning my back to him. So he can't see my face anymore.

So I don't see his and back down.

I feel him wait, hesitate behind me just as I feel the waves of gnawing worry roll off Cassian. But I don't look back. Not for either of them. I can't. If I look, I'm afraid that I will cave, crumple into the little girl that quaked under the covers as Az whispered stories in the dark of

4

the enkros and the terrible things they do to the draki they capture. We have no way of knowing for sure because none of those draki ever return home.

Finally, Will pushes the doors shut on me, sealing me in. I turn. For a moment, I press my trembling hands to the cold metal and hold them there, as if I can somehow reach him, feel him on the other side. *Him*. Not Cassian.

A moment later doors slam as Will and Cassian climb in up front. Then we're moving. The van rumbles all around me. I find a place to sit on the grimy floor and hug myself tightly, my stomach in knots.

Inhaling deep breaths, I wait for the van to stop and for it to begin—the battle I've waited my whole life to fight.

The bumpy ride strips away some of my courage. It's all so familiar that I question my sanity in volunteering to go through this again. The back of the van feels claustrophobic. Little air. No space to move. And I'm crippled. Hobbled like in my worst nightmares. My mind sticks on this, fastens on the memory of the last time I was a captive in a van like this. *Last time . . .*

It's the reason I'm here, after all.

I take small sips of air, fighting for calm and promising myself that I'm in control this time. Shaking my head, I swipe tangled strands of hair from my face and try to keep my balance as we take a sharp turn.

I make a mental list of the differences to steady my nerves. I trust the drivers. They have my back. I know where we're going—I've seen our destination. And I'm not in pain this time. At least not physically. But I'm also by myself. No Miram.

Miram is who we're doing this for—who we're saving. To be honest, she's only partly why I'm here. This has become something bigger, something more for me. A quest for truth. Will knows it. I don't think Tamra realizes, or even Cassian, but Will knows this is about finding answers. Finding Dad.

The van slows and stops. I hold my breath, air puffing from my lips and nose like fog. It's not deliberate. I can't help it—I am this: a creature that breathes fire. Right now emotion rules me, making it especially hard to be anything else.

Fear. Rage. Doubt. Was I kidding Will when I said this would work? Deluding myself? All of this rises inside me in a wash of char and cinder, ready to burst free in flame and fire.

Voices carry from outside my tin box. In moments I'll be on my own among the enkros. Just as planned. I wait, muscles tense and vibrating beneath my draki skin. My wings pull against their binding. Will did a good job. I couldn't break free if I wanted to. And I don't. That's not the plan. The plan is for me to play the role of a believable captive.

For a moment, I think of my sister alone in the motel room, waiting for the guys to return. She smiled when we parted ways, but the smile didn't reach her eyes. It wasn't in her heart. Moisture gleamed in her frost-coloured gaze and I know she broke down and cried as soon as we left.

Tamra was against this whole scheme as soon as I proposed it. Even after I persuaded Will and Cassian she continued to object. As the bindings dig into my flesh, cutting off my circulation, I shove aside thoughts of Tamra and my rising worries. With fresh resolve, I fix my gaze on the van's back doors and wait. Voices ride the air and I think I recognize the muffled sound of Will's voice.

Or it could just be that I want to hear him so much, so badly.

Cassian is there. I don't need to hear him to sense that. I can feel him. As I wait in shadow, his anger hits me like a fist, swift and fierce. He must be face-to-face with them now. A hissing breath escapes between my teeth as his rage suffuses me in a cold so deep it freeze-burns me to the marrow of my bones.

To combat this, I reach into myself for what I know— what I am. Heat swells up inside me, smoulders a path up my windpipe to war with Cassian's icy fury.

There's a clang and the scrape of metal on metal. I snap my gaze straight ahead, watching as the door opens.

Light floods my metal-walled cage and I lift my bound hands to shield my eyes. I peer through the cracks in my fingers and spot Will, looking relaxed and at ease, giving nothing away. At least outwardly. A muscle flickers, feathers the flesh of his jaw, signalling his tension to me even as he motions to me with his hand. 'There she is, boys . . .'

Cassian lingers a few feet behind him with several others—lab-coated individuals who peer at me with deep, measuring eyes. *Enkros*. This sight jars me. I couldn't have prepared for it.

Cassian. Standing with them. The irony isn't lost on me. A ridiculous urge to laugh bubbles up in my throat.

I force myself to focus. The van is backed in through some kind of garage door. A long narrow corridor of dull white stretches out before me. A single steel door waits at the far end. There's no possibility of escape to the outside world, to the sky. Not that I'm here to escape. Not yet anyway.

One of the lab coats steps forward. He holds a prod with a loop around the end. Before I realize what he's doing, he drops the stiff circle around my bound hands and cinches it tight, dragging me from the van with a rough yank. I catch only a glimpse of the man's determined eyes, so pale a blue they seem colourless, before I plunge from the van and hit the cold floor.

Landing on my shoulder, I cry out from the pain—all the while marvelling that these men should appear so *ordinary* in their lab coats. Like doctors or researchers, and not the secret menace that's shadowed my life for so long.

A fresh wave of Cassian's rage sweeps over me. I shudder and try to shake it off. It's debilitating—makes me want to fight, to unleash all that I am on these enkros. And I can't.

A sound escapes Will. Something between a grunt and a growl. When I glance up, my gaze collides with his. His hands flex at his sides. He's barely restraining himself. I give the barest shake of my head, hoping to communicate that he should hold himself in check.

They should go. I know this has to be killing them both and I can't risk either one of them showing the slightest sign that they're affected by my treatment.

'Get up! C'mon!' The guy yanks on the prod, and the binding cuts into my wrists so deeply I'm convinced if I don't move I might lose my hands.

Glaring at him, I'm struck by the dispassion in those pale blue eyes. There's nothing there—not even what I expected. None of the venom, none of the malice. *Because he's unbothered. He believes he's doing the right thing.*

Cassian's wrath continues winding its way through me.

'Look at her,' one of the lab coats exclaims. I'm almost tempted to look down at myself to see what he's talking about.

There's a rustle of quick, panicked movements, and then my mouth is sealed with duct tape before I even have time to react. I guess they know enough to know what I am. What I can do.

The lab coat stands back. 'There. That will do for now, until she's processed. She won't be lighting anyone up.'

Smothered, I grunt. My gaze swings wildly, searching for Will, needing to see him again, just once more before I'm taken away and 'processed'.

Another hard yank, and I scramble to my feet. I'm pulled forward quickly down the corridor, past the others. Caged bulbs of light emit a merciless yellow.

I'm moving. I can't see Will or Cassian any more.

But Cassian's fear and frustration still reach me. The blistering ice of those emotions wash over me. I look over my shoulder for a final glimpse of them.

Cassian stands statue-still, staring after me. Will is talking to one of the lab coats. His gaze slides to me once, briefly, and then away. He looks unusually pale, his hand chafing at the side of his neck as if there were something there he could rub out.

Then I reach the end of the hall. We're through the door and I can't see Will any more.

There is only what lies ahead of me now.

* * *

The elevator descends with me in it, surrounded by my captors. They hold themselves distant from me, hugging tight to the walls, weapons at the ready.

Even with my mouth taped, it's reassuring that they still consider me dangerous. I feel the absence of Will and Cassian as keenly as a knife's blade. Even as my heart longs for Will, it's Cassian's void I feel more intensely as his cold rage fades, departing with him. And it's not just his rage I lose. His concern, his worry and fear . . . his doubts. All that evaporates like smoke into the air.

Now it's just me with my feelings, but at least I no longer have to muddle through my emotions and struggle to separate what's me and what's Cassian.

I don't need to fake my fear as I'm led into the bowels of the stronghold. I'm not sure what I expected . . . maybe a castlelike dungeon? Either way, the white walls and brightly glowing ceiling aren't it. The tiled floor is chilly and smooth under my bare feet, and while I usually prefer the cold, I shiver. This is no cool forest floor, soft with pine needles and yielding soil. The sterile floor is hard and lifeless beneath me.

We approach a door that slides open silently from ceiling to floor.

I blink at the sudden glare of the room before me. As my eyes adjust to the light, my throat constricts at the sight that greets me.

A long observation table stretches before several cells. They all have Plexiglas fronts with three plain white walls. And inside each cell is a draki. All shapes, sizes, and colours.

I don't get an exact count. Maybe ten all together.

It's too much to take in and I can't move. I'm jabbed in the back so hard that I stagger. The lab coat in front of me shouts, his lips twisting in a snarl as he jerks on my wrists and pulls me up the moment before I fall to my knees.

Pain lances through the joints in my shoulders. The plastic ties tighten, cutting off my circulation.

I really am an animal to them. Less than that. A touch of disgust lurks in their eyes, but also a hint of fascination. For all that I'm a beast to them, I'm similar enough to them to creep them out. If I were just a simple animal, a common creature of the forest, they would treat me with more kindness and courtesy.

But I'm not.

I'm this alien thing to them, some freak they view as an anomaly even though my ancestors, dragons, have been here longer than man.

My heart beats a wild rhythm in my chest as I'm shoved forward into the wide room. I quickly scan each cell, not absorbing any draki individually in my search for Miram.

I spot her. My nostrils flare with excited breath to see her alive. She lies curled on her side, her tan, nondescript skin dull, not as vibrant as any of her neighbours. Her eyes are closed and her hair trails over the floor, lank and bland, like dried wheat.

I shout to her in our draki tongue. Despite the tape covering my mouth, I make a lot of noise. Several draki lift their heads in my direction.

But she doesn't react. Not even a flicker of her eyes.

I scream against my gag, saying her name over and over.

Her eyes flutter open, and I think she's heard me. She even looks in my direction. Then, no. Her lids close again. I deflate inside. It's like she doesn't care. Or maybe she can't process it's me. Maybe she's been drugged. Who knows what they've done to her.

Then I can no longer see her because I'm led to an empty cell. The Plexiglas slides open and I'm thrust inside. Several lab coats follow me. They stick me with a new prod and this one jolts me with an electrical current.

I drop, dead weight, choke on a scream. They make quick work of unbinding my wings and wrists as I twitch on the cold floor, able to see and feel but unable to control my movements. In short, hell. They leave the duct tape over my mouth, but I lack the strength to rip it free.

All of them leave my cell except one. He lingers, staring at me with mild interest. My pulse stutters against my neck as I endure his scrutiny, knowing he can do anything to me and I can't lift a finger to help myself.

He bends down and strokes my arm with a slow drag of fingers that makes my stomach twist sickly. Scalding bile rises to the back of my throat.

Another lab coat appears behind him. 'C'mon, Lewis.'

Lewis shakes his head, musing, 'This one sure has pretty skin.' He watches me with cold curiosity.

'Yeah, and she breathes fire, so if I were you, I'd get out of here until we've studied her properly and know how to deal with this particular dragon. Remember the stories from those hunters who last captured a fire-breather?'

'Think this is the same one?'

'Dunno. Doesn't matter. My point is she escaped them. Don't underestimate this one. Now, c'mon.' The lab coat dispensing advice moves away.

Lewis continues to watch me, his head cocked at an angle. 'Yeah. But you can't do anything right now, can you? You're harmless.' His hand glides over my belly. He palms my flesh leisurely before his fingers grab and pinch me, twisting my skin with swift savagery. 'How does it feel to be defenceless? You're at our mercy now. There's no escape. Understand?'

After a long moment, he gives a satisfied nod and releases me. 'See you later.' He steps back several paces until the Plexiglas slides shut between us.

Alone, I lie still and press my trembling lips shut. It's all I can do not to scream.

CHAPTER TWO

I lie on the floor, shaking, my belly still throbbing from where the bastard hurt me. The effects of the electric jolt gradually fade from my limbs and I clutch my knees close to my chest, staring vaguely at the enkros moving back and forth outside my cell. Is this what happened to Dad? Was he here? I didn't have time to see much before they forced me into the cell. If I called out 'Magnus', would he answer me?

The ghostly, white-coated figures shuffle around, pre-occupied with their tasks. Minutes pass before I feel ready to move again. Uncurling, I push up with my palms, my muscles trembling from the effort.

I catch a voice, a draki whispering softly from some-where to my right. I strain to hear beyond the faint clicking of computer keys and the hum of human voices at the observation table. Two enkros sit there, looking up occasionally. Sometimes at me, sometimes at the other cells. I would bet someone sits there at all times, watch-ing, studying us for anything the cameras in the corners might miss. I hate this. That I can never make a move without being noticed.

I begin to piece together the words drifting through the wall. *Iwanttogohomelwanttogohomelwanttogohomeplease* . . .

It's a female draki, and I can't help but wonder if she isn't a little insane. Who knows how long she's been here. How long any of them have been captives.

I shiver and quickly remind myself that I only have to survive one day. I can do this. Twenty-four hours and Will and Cassian will come for me. This reminder works—brings me back to my purpose.

I rise, ignore the eyes watching me, the camera lens recording my every move. My fingers grasp the edges of the duct tape covering my mouth and peel it free in one burning rip. I wince and drag in air through my tender lips.

'Miram!' I call hoarsely at first, then again, firmer, beating the glass with the flat of my palm.

The enkros watch me, but I ignore them, knowing that they can't understand me.

'Miram, it's me, Jacinda! Don't worry, Miram. I'm here to rescue you.'

Nothing. Just the girl next door to me muttering her endless mantra. I stop myself from shouting at her to shut up.

'Miram, can you hear me? Please say something. Cassian sent me. He's here, too. Just outside. We're here to get you out!'

Nothing. I thought the mention of her brother would rouse her as nothing else could. That's why I came in. Aside from being here so Cassian can locate us via his connection to me, I'm here to warn Miram . . . to prepare her for the breakout.

With these urgent thoughts in my mind, I press on. I have to try.

'Miram,' I shout. 'You don't have to answer me, but be ready. We're busting you out of here. In the next twenty-four hours, we're escaping. Be ready for it.'

Laughter carries from the cell to my left. Draki laughter. The lab coats on duty seem fascinated by the growling bursts of sound. They fall into a flurry of activity, documenting the strange sounds. Of course. They probably haven't heard much laughter within these walls.

The sound grates. I press my hands against the wall I share with the laughing draki. 'What's so funny?' I hiss.

The laughter only continues.

I cover my hands over my ears. 'Enough already!'

Suddenly the laughter stops. I lift my hands. For a moment, I think I won't be answered; then suddenly the guttural tones of a male draki scrape the air. 'That you think you'll ever get out of here alive. *That* I find highly amusing.'

At these words my bravado wavers. I manage to snatch it back and demand through the wall, 'So what? You don't have any hope at all? You've just quit? Accepted your lot in here?'

'No, I haven't quit.' He sounds indignant now. Better that than the draki on the other side of me that sounds half mad with incessant whispering. 'I'm just trying to stay sane and alive down here. The friend you're calling— Miram? She gave up a long time ago.'

I shake my head. 'You're content to live out your days here?'

'It's living.'

'Hardly. We're breaking out of here,' I vow. 'Just watch.'

The grating laughter returns. 'Well, if that happens, I'll be close on your heels.'

I lower back to the cold floor, resting my legs that still feel as insubstantial as jelly. I eye what I can see of the room on the other side of the Plexiglas: the long observation desk, various cameras positioned at every corner. The few enkros in the room talk in low voices. They seem to be in the process of deciding something. One lab coat glances at his watch and motions to all of us lined up in our cells. Another lab coat looks at me pointedly and shakes his head, clearly disagreeing about something.

I lean to the side until my shoulder touches the Plexiglas. I try to decipher their muffled voices, sure that whatever they're talking about has to do with me. I need to be ready.

More enkros arrive, and the ones behind the observation table practically bow and scrape before them.

I'm taking it all in, when another draki speaks, her young voice carrying from a couple cells over.

'If *they* don't get you, the grey one will.'

She sounds just like a child, I think, angling my head. 'What do you mean?'

'If the enkros don't finish you, then he will.' She pronounces *he* like I should understand her meaning. 'The grey one.'

'Who's the "grey one"?'

'Oh, he's mean. He's been here longer than any of us.' She makes a sniffing sound. 'Probably why he's so nasty. You gotta stay away from him.'

'What is he?' I've never heard of a grey draki before. He must possess a talent I don't know about. Instead of fear, excitement quivers through me . . . to meet other draki, learn about a draki I never even knew existed. It's not something I considered coming here. Too many other thoughts consumed me.

'You better hope you don't find out. Just stay out of his way. Hide.'

I'm about to ask when I would supposedly meet this draki—we're kept in these cells, after all—when a low siren begins to ring and a flashing red light suffuses the room.

'What's going on?' I demand, looking around wildly.

Even from my cell, I can hear the draki scrambling to their feet. In the back of my mind, I wonder if Miram moves, too. Or is she still a lump on the floor of her cell?

'Get ready!' the male draki who spoke to me commands.

Ready? Ready for what?

Even so, my muscles tighten and bunch beneath my flesh. Suddenly the back side of my cell slides open. The wall isn't a wall at all. It just drops down into the floor like a car window, revealing a lush world of vegetation.

There are several whooshes of wind as other draki flee through the air and disappear into the thick vegetation. They're gone in a blink, ghosts on the air, lost in foliage humming with life, too fast for me to process them or identify if Miram is among them.

I edge forward carefully, not sure what to expect. As soon as I clear the threshold of my cell, it slides shut after me. No going back.

I release a breath slowly, flexing my bare feet in the soil. It's just me. No other draki in sight. Not even useless curled-up-in-a-ball Miram. But I know they're all out there, in this vast simulation of a forest.

What are the enkros doing? What are they hoping to accomplish? I glance around, scanning the thick press of trees, and that's when I spot them. Cameras. Everywhere. Perched high in the leaves of a tree. In the knothole of a trunk. I doubt there is an inch of this mock forest they cannot see.

Which makes me wonder what they're expecting to film. Us interacting? Because as far as I can tell, no one is interacting. Everyone is . . . hiding.

At this realization everything inside of me seizes up. I remember the warning about the grey draki.

Stay away from him . . .

Out of his way . . .

Hide . . .

Just like everyone is doing now. Except me. Suddenly I know I shouldn't be standing out in the open like this. Too late, a growl rumbles across the crisp air, and a second realization steals over me.

I'm not alone.

He's grey. Just like the draki girl described. A slate grey like liquid steel, quite possibly the largest draki I've ever seen. He stands taller than the onyx back home. He's obviously strong. Maybe fast, too. His wings are leathery, but an ashy colour, spearing the air high above his massive shoulders. I don't think he's old, but then there's something about his eyes . . . that pewter gaze contains such cunning, a savage menace that seems ancient.

Suddenly, I wish I'd asked more questions, demanded more answers from the girl when she'd been offering her advice.

'Hi,' I say, holding myself still, unsure what to do. My fingers tap my thighs in agitation. I've never come face-to-face with a draki who didn't belong to my pride before. Historically, prides are fractious, warring tribes. That's what led to the last Great War.

The old texts chronicled several hundred prides, too many to know for certain. We learned about them in school. I'd even read about some of the history in our librarian Taya's tomes, fascinated with the time before the wars when the prides were united as one great nation.

As I stare at him, I accept that it shouldn't be a shock to meet a new draki. I've always known they're out there.

But it *is* a big deal. Every fibre of my being pulses with the instinct to fight, to defend. It's the same reaction I had when the hunters pursued me, but I never thought I'd feel this way around another draki. It seems somehow sacrilegious. We're the same, after all.

Oh, sure, there are the troublemakers like Miram, and even those that make me feel intimidated like Severin and Corbin. But facing off with this draki . . . this is different.

Now, in this moment, I feel as though my next move will signify life or death for me.

He doesn't respond to my greeting. Ash and char rise in my throat and my muscles twist tighter, ready to spring into action.

Facing him, I'm reminded of a prison movie I watched long ago, lodged deep in my memory. It's a strange sense of déjà vu. Like I'm cast into that movie. I'm the new inmate, standing in the yard, squaring off with the established bully.

I try to remember what the newbie did to survive because, of course, he's the hero who makes it to the end. Just like I intend to. Or at least through the next twenty-four hours until my friends break us out of here.

'I don't want any trouble,' I say.

The draki makes a strange noise, a guttural rattling sound in his throat that I've never heard from another draki before, and I wonder if it's some kind of battle call. As I watch him, his scaly flesh seems to undulate and shiver.

'W-what are you doing?' I ask, knowing it could be anything. I don't know what power he possesses. Whatever it is, it's enough to send other draki into hiding.

I slide back a step over the moist ground, my gaze fastened on him, afraid to look away.

Suddenly his scales flip *up*. Every inch of him is covered in sharp-edged disks perpendicular to his massive body. They glint razor-sharp and I know one brush against him will cut me to ribbons.

My stomach drops. In a flash of clarity, I know why the others fled the minute the doors slid open.

With a muttered curse, I swing around and push off the ground in one smooth move, deciding that the others had the right idea. I need to get away from this draki. Fast.

Instantly, I'm lost in the roar of wind as I whip through the bramble of trees. I hear him crashing behind me. I'm quick but so is he. *Go, go, go, go* pants from my lips in an endless mantra.

The idea of him catching me, slamming his razor-sharp body into mine, fills me with a fear so intense that fire builds in my lungs and coats my mouth. And I know there is no choice. I have to stand and defend myself.

I stop mid-air and twirl around, my wings great flapping sails behind me—but nothing like his that tear through the air, creating sharp drafts of wind that rip the leaves from the trees.

As he comes at me, I build and gather the heat inside me, knowing that no little warning puff of steam will suffice. For him, I need fire. Killing flames.

When he's close—his face so near I can see the hard, relentless lines of his features, the ridged nose and flaring nostrils—I release the tremendous burn of heat from inside me.

It bursts forth in a maelstrom of angry, crackling flame.

He drops to the side and under me, narrowly missing the full brunt.

I spin, looking beneath me, and see him coming back, surging straight up. The gleam in his eyes tells me he's not intimidated by my talent. If anything, it gratifies him.

Maybe that freaks me out the most. Fire doesn't scare him? Does he want to be burned? Does he have a death wish?

Realizing I know nothing about how this draki will react, I dive, fly low to the ground, looking over my shoulder. And, yes, he's behind me again, relentlessly pursuing me. I don't stop this time. I shoot fire backward, over my shoulder.

He swerves in my trail, determined to catch me. It's like there isn't anything but the savage inside him, the dragon of old, not a shred of humanity. He wants to destroy me.

My teeth clamp hard in my mouth and I push myself faster.

My thoughts race. I know what I have to do. I drop until I touch down, and then I flip onto my back and wait, the smoulder brewing inside me, the grass soft and yielding beneath me as I stare at the draki coming at me. Steam escapes from my nose. His gaze follows that steam before locking with my eyes. There's satisfaction in that gleaming pewter . . . and I get the sneaking suspicion that this satisfaction is not because he's convinced that he's about to kill me. *No. He wants me to win.* He wants me to beat him. So he'll be free of this place.

Just as he's about to reach me, we're swarmed.

The enkros invade the simulated forest, a dozen of them garbed head to toe in white suits that make them look like spacemen. I'm grabbed by the arms and dragged away. I struggle—it's my instinct to do so. Even if they are rescuing me from some hell-bent killer draki. Or rescuing him from me. I'm not sure which is the case.

'What are you doing?' I shout at them. 'Isn't this what you wanted? Don't you want us to kill each other? C'mon! C'mon!' I thrash in their arms, blowing fire that does nothing as it bounces off their fire-resistant suits.

Several of them surround the grey draki. Even in their suits, they don't lay a hand on him, and I guess it's because he'd rip straight through the special material of their protective gear.

They stab him with a sharp stick—and then I realize it's no stick. It's an electric rod like the one they used on me. However it doesn't seem to have any effect on him.

23

Maybe it doesn't penetrate? Or maybe he's just too strong to care?

And it's there, rising inside me, unbelievable maybe, but true nonetheless. Pity.

He snarls and growls, howling as they stab him repeatedly. Yet he never drops. He's been Tased again and again and it doesn't faze him.

God, what *is* he?

Then I'm back in my cell and the wall is sliding shut, sealing me in. I'm all alone, shuddering with great smoking breaths.

And I can't see anything any more.

CHAPTER THREE

'Hey, Jacinda!' The loud whisper penetrates my fog of thoughts. It's the young female draki who spoke to me before. 'You OK in there?'

Lying sideways on the floor, still dazed from my brush with death, I crack one eye open. The fight with a kamikaze draki left me shaken, inside and out. Physically drained. Mentally exhausted. And I haven't even been here an hour. Or have I? Every moment drags on in agony.

I sit up slowly, rubbing the side of my face. 'Yeah. I'm fine. What's your name?' I ask, figuring it's time I knew.

The voice calls to me again. 'I'm Lia.' Even through the walls I can hear her youth and innocence. 'I've never met a fire-breather before.'

I don't bother pointing out that we haven't actually met. 'No? What kind of draki are you?'

'I'm a water draki. For about six months anyway.'

A water draki like Az. A pang strikes near my heart as I think of my friend back home. I remind myself that

25

this isn't the end, even though in just a short amount of time, this world, my role as a captive, has consumed me. It feels like everything. It feels as though I've been stuck down here for days. What must it be like for the others who've been trapped so much longer? I remember the grey draki . . . the hunger for death in his eyes, and I guess I know what it would be like. Then Lia's last words sink in. Six months?

'How old are you?' I ask.

'Twelve.'

Twelve! Just a baby. 'How long have you been here?

'A couple of months now.' She says this so matter-of-factly that I shudder. If possible, the walls suddenly seem closer, tighter all around me. I rub hard at my temples. 'Sorry I didn't warn you better about the grey one—'

I shake my head before remembering she can't see me through the cell walls. 'You tried. There wasn't much time to explain.'

'There never is.'

'What do you mean?'

'The first thing they do when they capture a new draki is throw all of us together in the Wood. That's where they keep *him*.' I know who she means now. 'They want to see how each new draki acts in the general population. Well, they mostly want to see how a new draki reacts to the grey. You know, if we have a good talent or not.'

'What is he? Where does he come from?'

'He's not like any of us.'

'Considering his first impulse is to try to annihilate his own kind? Yeah. Kind of figured that.'

The male draki on the other side of me interjects with, 'He's old. Older than all of us.'

'He didn't look that old,' I say.

'My guess is he's the oldest of any living draki. More dragon than human.'

I frown. 'How do you know this?'

'Roc knows everything. He's really smart,' Lia pipes in.

'It's just a theory,' Roc says. 'As time passes, we've become more and more human. I'm guessing we used to be more like him . . . more dragon. He's what we were.' He pauses and I can almost envision the draki shrugging on the other side of the wall. 'He's what we were maybe a couple of thousand years ago. Before civilization took hold. Primitive. Savage.'

I bite my lip. Maybe. But I also wondered if he was vicious as a result of what the enkros did to him. Maybe he's just been driven crazy by captivity. Even now I can feel myself fraying at the edges.

I swallow and shake my head. I'm not here to solve the riddle of the grey draki. I'm here to rescue Miram and hopefully, in the process, bring down this entire operation. End these enkros that may have had something to do with taking Dad from me. Even if they didn't, they need to be stopped.

Silence descends around me and I know we're mulling over our own thoughts. Somewhere in the distance, down the row of cells, I hear a voice muttering in the draki tongue. The humans at the observation desk talk in a low dull drone. One of them catches me watching him and I look away, too uncomfortable to hold his gaze, as though he might be able to see inside me to my secrets.

Restless, I pace the short length of floor, wondering

how much time has passed since I've been in this cell. Already it feels too long. I'm not made for this—to be penned in. Not that anyone is, but I feel especially on edge. Like I might pull out my hair if I don't escape from this box soon.

'Miram,' I call out after several moments, determined to try again. 'Are you there?'

Of course, she's here. Where would she have gone?

'I know you're there,' I assert. 'And I know you're mad at me.' Even apart from our mission to rescue her, somehow it's become important to put things right between us. Ever since I bonded with Cassian, my feelings toward her just aren't so . . . *hard*. I'm certain feeling Cassian's emotions, his love and affection for his sister, have influenced me.

'Mad?' The familiar voice finally cracks across the air. 'Why would I be mad? You only got me captured by hunters and thrown into this hell!'

I suck in a deep breath and resist telling her the fault is as much hers as mine. She shouldn't have been following me and spying on me in the first place! But I'm not here to argue with her. I have to make her see that—to see that we're allies.

'Your brother is here, Miram.'

A long pause follows before: 'Cassian?'

'Yeah.'

'He's come for me?'

'Yes. We all have. Tamra too. I got caught so Cassian can find us once they get inside.' I swallow. 'We've bonded. He'll know right away where I am. We're going to break you out.' I don't mention Will. Considering Miram wouldn't escape with me the last time because

Will was there with me, I think it's best to leave off mentioning him for now.

All the draki around me are quiet and I know Miram isn't the only one listening. They're absorbing my words just as much as she is. I would be doing the same thing—my thoughts would be racing as to whether I could be free as well.

'All of you,' I call out. 'We're all escaping this place.'

'Oh, thank you,' Lia cries excitedly.

Roc just mutters, 'We'll see,' but I can hear a faint thread of hope in his voice.

'What do I need to do to help?' Miram asks.

My shoulders sag, relieved at her words—that she's on board. 'Be ready. Follow my lead no matter what.' *Even when you see Will.* 'It can't be like last time,' I warn. 'No panicking . . .'

'I'll be ready.' There's a whisper of anger in her voice and I figure this is OK. Even a good thing. A little anger is healthy. Maybe it will give her courage when the time to act arrives.

I slide down, the wall at my back.

And then that draki starts up again with her maddening chants. Apparently my promise for escape didn't register with her. The words run together so quickly now that I can't even make them out. I press both hands over my ears to try and block out her shrill voice. Impossible.

Roc bellows at her and I jump. She doesn't let up though. If anything she grows louder. Another sound joins in the cacophony. The sound of someone beating the walls. It almost sounds like a body crashing against a cell.

The force sends a vibration through the floor that travels up my legs.

I bury my face in my hands, convinced I've just plunged into an asylum. Just one day. *Just one day.*

Time can't move fast enough.

CHAPTER FOUR

My gaze grows blurry as I stare too long out of the Plexiglas. I blink my aching eyes and look away, trying to focus my thoughts again. Hard. Impossible. My adrenalin gone, I feel almost ill, drained and sickly lethargic. A dull ache throbs at the back of my head, gnawing at me like some kind of beast working on a bone. I rub a hand at the base of my skull. I can't find myself anywhere amid the whirling buzz of my thoughts. All my confidence eludes me. Yes. We have a plan, but what if it doesn't work? What if Will, Cassian, and Tamra try to rescue us and fail? What if I'm stuck here? Locked in a cell forever? Panic claws its way up my throat.

Cassian. My mind whispers his name, searching for him, trying to reach him. Can he feel me? Hear me?

Cassian, I don't know how much longer I can stand this. I think the words, form them in my head like I'm talking to him, like he's there, inside me.

For the first time I need the bond between us to work.

He's my only connection to the outside. To life away from here. *To Will.*

A lab coat strolls past and backs up, stopping in front of my cell with a suddenness that makes me recoil.

He holds a clipboard in one hand and a sandwich in the other, an abundance of lettuce sticking out from all sides of the bread. He watches me with a curious fascination—as though I might suddenly do something of interest. Or I already am . . .

He taps on the Plexiglas with one finger, smudging the surface with a streak of mustard.

'Hi, there.' He coos at me like I'm a pet to tame. 'Aren't you a pretty girl?'

I angle my head. My chest expands, swells with heat. Steam puffs from my nose as I watch him. He chuckles.

Another enkros steps up beside him. 'She's something. Think we'll get to cut this one open? Be interesting to see how the lungs and airways function.'

'I imagine it will come to that eventually.' He takes a bite from his sandwich and talks with his mouth full. 'After we've run all our evaluations. We've never had one like her. Doc will want a look inside.'

I rise to my feet. Their faces sway as I stagger my way toward them. Unable to stop myself, I strike the glass with my fist. It shudders beneath the force but doesn't give. Not that I expected it to.

They smile, amused by my outburst.

'I think she understands us.' Sandwich Eater nods as though convinced and then sets his sandwich on the bottom half of the clipboard so he can scribble a note of my behaviour. 'The doctor will be pleased. He always credits them with intelligence.'

The other lab coat snorts and shakes his head. 'They're just animals. Fascinating creatures, sure, but they understand about as much as my Labrador.'

They move away then.

I pace my prison and try to reach Cassian again, desperate, unable to shake off the panic that I'll never be rescued from this cell.

I drag my hands through my hair and fall against the wall. Hot tears slip down my cheeks. Sliding to the floor, I release a great gust of breath and close my eyes, fighting back the emotion. No tears. I won't let them see me weep so they can write that down in their reports.

Cassian. Help me. Help Miram.

Dropping my head onto my knees, I sink into the dark shell of myself, not expecting the scene awaiting me there.

A hazy image fills my mind. It's daylight. Outdoors. I see my sister and Will. He's pacing near the van.

I open my eyes in a flash and find myself still in my cell. Even hazy, the image had seemed so real.

Lowering my head, I close my eyes again and I'm sucked back into the misty vision. With Will and Tamra. But where's Cassian?

Will charges towards me, his face tight and anxious, his chest taut beneath the T-shirt that he'd been wearing when we parted. My heart swells, overcome at the sight of him.

'Do you feel her? How is she? Does she want us to come?'

Then I understand. I've succeeded in reaching out to Cassian. Beyond my wildest imaginings, I've connected to him. So much so that I'm *in* him right now. I can feel and see everything he's experiencing.

Cassian's voice rises up from inside me—or rather inside him. 'Yes. I feel her. She's not . . . managing it very well.'

'Are they harming her?' Will demands. His skin pales, eyes strained and unblinking as he stares at Cassian.

'I don't think so,' Cassian answers. 'Not now, anyway. I don't sense any pain. But . . .'

'Is she scared?' Tamra asks.

My vision bounces as Cassian nods.

Tamra moistens her lips. 'Then do something for her. You can reach her. Comfort her . . .'

Will's expression is wild. 'We need to go in. We can't wait.' Before anyone can answer, he curses and moves away, prowling out of Cassian's sight. My sister starts to follow him but pauses and turns back to Cassian.

The connection begins to fade, but I'm comforted. Relieved. It can't be much longer. They'll come for us.

Exhausted, I fall asleep again and dream of Will.

It's not the first time he's filled my dreams, but it's the first time he's flying beside me as a draki. His eyes are the same but for the fully vertical pupils. They glow with delight as we soar and dip, cutting through the wet kiss of clouds. His skin is iridescent, flashing from gold to brown to green—just like his hazel eyes. His wings move fluidly on the air, great sails whooshing beside me. When I wake, I feel the irrational urge to cry as reality slams down on me.

Tears burn the backs of my eyes. Because Will flying— that can never be. The sweetness of those moments found in sleep will never happen. He and I can never have that, be together that way, as two draki. Even if he's proven to be something else, something more than human, he can never take to the skies with me.

And does he have to? a small voice whispers inside my head. *You never cared about that before.*

I pull my knees to my chest and chafe my supple skin with both hands. Maybe being here, a prisoner of men, allied only with fellow draki (except the one, of course, that would prefer to kill me) and longing for the sky, I'm feeling the gulf between Will and myself more sharply.

The door of the observation room opens. More lab coats pour inside. They're pushing a sheet-covered gurney with brown leather straps dangling off the sides. The sight of it starts a slow, nervous fluttering in my stomach.

I rise to my feet, my heart rate increasing. I back against a wall, pressing my palms into the cold concrete. A draki somewhere down the line begins making a racket. Almost like he's digging at the concrete floor.

'What's going on?' I call out, hoping one of them will answer me.

Lia obliges—her tone apologetic—as if she were somehow responsible. 'They've come for you. It's your turn.'

I gasp. 'My turn for what?'

'At the beginning, they take each of us . . . put something inside of us.'

'What *thing?*' I shout, pacing rapidly inside my cell, back and forth, back and forth, as if my quick movements can somehow carry me away from all this.

'I don't know really . . . some little shiny metal thing. It hurts only for a second.'

Shiny metal thing?

I flatten my palms against the wall again and shake my head from side to side as if I can will it all to stop, will the enkros not to come for me. I hadn't anticipated this. I didn't think they would have time to do anything *bad* to me before I was rescued.

'No point fighting it,' Roc volunteers, his voice grim. 'We all have to go through it.'

We all have to go through it.

Somehow that doesn't hearten me. Terror rises up my throat as I watch the humans stop on the other side of my Plexiglas cell. I'm not supposed to go through this. Just twenty-four hours. That was the plan. Not this. This was never the plan. And now it's supposed to be sooner. Will said they were coming. Where are they? Did something go wrong?

I might have been the pliable creature before, when I first arrived and was playing a role, but I can't afford to be that easy victim any longer. I can't be anything but myself.

I'm ready for them when they crack open the Plexiglas. I blast a path of crackling fire, intent on keeping them from reaching me.

They back away at first, but then come again, crouching low. Several times they try, edging carefully into the cell. Each time I reward them with fire, pushing them back out.

I pant loudly, hot smoky breath falling from my lips. I refuse to wonder how long I can keep this up. I just tell myself I must. I have to last until Will gets here.

Their faces are angry and red as they slide the Plexiglas closed and regroup. They glare at me, their determination to have me, get me, break me, no less bright in their eyes.

'She was easy before,' one says, his voice very close to a whine.

Easy? Right.

One finally orders, 'Enough of this. Go suit up.'

My stomach clenches and I know what *suits* he's talking about. The fire-resistant ones they wore into the simulated forest to stop the grey one and me from killing each other.

Two suited men return. Apparently they thought two would be enough to handle me. I tense, my thighs quivering in readiness. A low growl swells from my throat.

The others step back as the two suited men square off in front of my cell, each holding the cattle prods I remember so well from when I first arrived.

The Plexiglas slides open again and I blast them with fire, following the trail of flames. I surge between their bodies, intent on escape.

I can't get past them though. They zing me. My every muscle seizes as the electric current runs through me. A scream strangles and locks in my throat. I can't move. No matter how my mind commands my body to move, to *go*—I can't.

I drop to my knees, the impact jarring me deep to the bones. Someone's behind me. I hear the loud peeling of tape. A hand grabs a fistful of my hair and forces my head back. My scalp burns.

Spots dance before my eyes.

It's the duct tape again, flattened over my mouth.

He releases my hair and I drop forward, dead weight. I will myself to move, to rise. Nothing.

They don't bother to bind my wings. Nor do they tie my wrists. I guess after that electric jolt, they're not too worried about me lashing out. Two men grab my arms and drag me. My feet twitch, struggling to push flat in order to gain purchase on the slick tiles.

The room spins. Faces fly past. People. Like me. I want to shout, *I'm like you! You're hurting someone who does all the things, big and small, that you do. Someone who thinks and lives and loves and hates. And hates . . .*

Hates all of you.

Fire burns through me like a fast-spreading disease. My lips tingle beneath the smothering tape.

They fling me on the gurney like I'm nothing. Already dead. A corpse. Except if I were a corpse they wouldn't care to do whatever horrible things they have planned. They wouldn't need to stick some shiny metallic thing inside me.

My mind whirls, brain racing wildly, trying to think what it could be. What it will do to me.

They strap me in, bear me down with leather straps fastened at my ankles and wrists.

And as if that were not enough, a leather band stretches across my chest and hips. They adjust it, squeeze and pull so tightly I can hardly breathe through my nose. I begin to feel dizzy.

One of the lab coats peers down at me. 'She's strong. Make sure they're tight.' He frowns and resets his glasses on the bridge of his nose. 'You sure she can't burn through the tape?'

'She didn't last time.'

Fools. I didn't try the last time. Now I have to try.

I gather up the smoulder from deep in my chest, let it rise. I push the scald up my windpipe and try to let it fill my mouth, but it doesn't work. It's not right. The tape is too constrictive. I can't work my facial muscles, can't

38

get my mouth wide enough. Frustration burns a different kind of fire through me. Helpless rage.

I can't flex my cheeks like I need to. I can't even part my lips wide enough.

Desperate now, I struggle against my leather straps. Useless.

One of the lab coats smooths a hand over my sweaty brow. 'Easy there, girl.'

Like I'm some dog to be soothed. If I had use of my mouth I'd spit on him. Wait—no. Burn him to a crisp. It's what I'm born to do. Why the pride always thought I was so important. But I'm not. I can't even help myself. I turn my head, shaking off his touch. He clucks his tongue and glances at the others.

He continues in that placating tone, 'This will help us to take care of you, make sure you're safe . . .'

I try to guess what that means. Is it some kind of implant to monitor my vitals? To what extent I can't guess. Who knows what technology they're capable of? All I know is that I don't want it in me. I *can't* let them put it in me.

'She's feisty. This one is going to need serious management.'

'If anyone can do it you can. You've got such a tender way with them.'

Soft chuckles accompany me as I'm wheeled from the room, and I know that the last thing this guy has is a tender hand.

I crane my head and try to follow the direction we take down halls, which blur past me, try to spot any ways out of here. We travel a long distance and then turn left. From there we don't go very far.

I'm pushed through a set of double swinging doors that remind me of the ones in hospital emergency rooms you see on TV. The inside of the room is just as sterile and unfriendly as an operating room.

I'm rolled to the centre of the room beneath several blinding-bright lights. Other lab coats wait here. I glimpse a wide rectangular window to my right. Several people crowd in there, more lab coats and even some ordinary-looking people, dressed like civilians.

They peer through the glass curiously, like spectators at a circus come to witness the freak. And I guess that's all I am to them. My head turns anxiously, taking it all in, helpless but still searching, scanning for a way out of this.

I look up at the lab coat examining me. He's old. Older than any other enkros I've seen. The hair is so white and sparse on his head that I can see the paper-thin skin of his scalp.

His touch on my arm is cold. He squeezes a bit as though testing the texture and density of me.

Terror holds me, twists around my heart, and . . . and then something else intrudes. A growing thread of emotion weaves through me. The emotion spirals from a gnawing ache nibbling at my mind to a powerful wrench in my gut. It's worry. Plain and simple. Only it's not coming from me . . . *it's not me at all.*

My every nerve bursts, overcome and slammed with a sudden onslaught of emotions.

His name shudders through me in a sigh. *Cassian.* He's close. His worry and anxiety wash over me in prickles that flash cold and hot. Are they coming? I come alive with this possibility. Suddenly I don't feel so wretchedly alone strapped down to this table.

With a new burst of energy, I focus on the old man above me and the way the scalpel glints with menace in the unforgiving light. His gloved hand trails up my neck, leaving a wake of gooseflesh.

'Now,' he murmurs, 'let's see.' His fingers turn my head and feel their way through my hair, stopping above my ear.

I struggle, turning in the opposite direction. My head is forced back into place with hard hands as a thick leather strap is pulled tight across my forehead, cutting into my skin.

The old man's touch grows firmer as he delves between my strands of hair . . . looking for something, it seems, on my scalp. 'This spot looks perfect,' he announces.

Two other lab coats peer behind him, observing his ministrations. The old man glances over his shoulder, his every motion impatient and annoyed. 'Jenkins?'

'Yes, Doctor,' a voice replies in absolute deference.

A loud whirring fills the air. It's an angry sound, alive and threatening. I can't move my head. My eyes roll wildly, trying to see what it is.

Jenkins appears next to the doctor, a shaver in his hand.

I moan against the tape as the cold teeth of the shaver are pressed to my scalp, just above my ear. In a mere moment, a small place is shaved clean. A tuft of red-gold hair floats before my eyes. Then there is silence as the device is shut off.

'There we go.' The doctor slides his spectacles farther up his thin nose.

Jenkins takes the shaver and steps hurriedly to the side, just out of my vision. He returns with a pair of tongs that hold a patch of gauze. The cotton is stained a yellow-orange with some kind of ointment. 'Here you go, Doctor.'

He takes the tongs and lowers the gauze to my head.

I cringe, unsure what it is, but brace for discomfort. The gauze hits me, cold and wet, but painless. He brushes it against the naked flesh of my scalp in several sweeps.

'Almost ready.' The doctor hands the tongs back and returns into my line of sight with a scalpel in his hand. I inhale a sharp breath through my nose. He doesn't speak, simply frowns as he concentrates on my head.

'This will just hurt a pinch.' His gaze cuts to mine and fixes for a moment, and I wonder if he suspects that I can understand him.

I jerk against the strap holding my head down, straining my neck.

'It will hurt more if you move.' He holds my stare with those chilly eyes of his for a long moment, and there's no wondering. He doesn't think I understand him. He *knows*. And this only makes him more of a monster. Defeat spreads through me.

He gives a nod, satisfied I won't jerk around on the gurney anymore. And I won't. The last thing I want is for him to slit my throat or lop off my ear.

The blade lowers.

This is the part where I hold my breath and tell myself those swinging doors will fling open with Will and Cassian and Tamra. That they'll charge inside the room and cut me free of the straps restraining me. Will's arms will wrap around me. His lips will press to mine.

That's the way it should happen. That's the way it's *supposed* to happen.

Only it doesn't.

CHAPTER FIVE

The doctor cuts me, pushing the blade deep into my skin, passing through tissue. Warm blood oozes free, trickling through my hair. I cry out into the tape, the sound a muffled screech. Fire burns up my throat, an automatic defence that does me no good now. Smoky air rushes from my nostrils.

He slices. I know it only takes seconds, but it feels like forever. Like everything else down here, the sharp pressure stretches infinitely.

I glance at him as he straightens up, fingers curled around the scalpel. My blood coats its silver surface, a glittery purple in the bright light, proclaiming my heritage. He quickly hands off the knife and then presses a small vial against the stinging gash in my scalp, collecting the blood.

'Not a drop wasted,' he murmurs.

That done, he accepts a new item from Jenkins. A small metal disk, no bigger than my fingernail.

He moves slowly now, carefully, his movements precise and practised as he handles the tiny disk, and I can't help wondering if Dad lay on this same gurney, a small metal disk poised over him.

Suddenly my panic ebbs into something calmer. I feel oddly at peace. Like Cassian is beside me, whispering encouragement.

And I know I can't have that thing inside me. I struggle again, trying to pull away, but there's no give in my restraints. Nowhere to go.

I cringe and strain against the straps. His rubbery grip curves against my skull. I whimper, nostrils flaring rapidly with hot puffs of breath as he stretches the incision he made wider, lowering the tiny little metal disk toward me, bringing it down so that I can't see it any more.

Suddenly the lights flicker and flash. The doctor pauses, looks up with a frown. Jenkins murmurs something unintelligible and looks all around, his eyebrows drawing together.

And then the lights go out and we're plunged into blackness.

The darkness lasts only a moment. Just long enough for one of the lab coats to expel a curse. But enough time for me to feel the tension sweep over the enkros.

A layer of fear drapes the room. The backup lights flicker on. A dull red glow suffuses the air, reminding me of blood. Human blood, of course. It colours everything. Turns their white coats pink. Paints the strained faces of my captors a demonic red.

'W-what is it?' Jenkins practically whispers.

The doctor shakes his head. 'Probably just a drill—'

'And no one alerted us?'

The doctor frowns, his caterpillar eyebrows drawing

together tighter, and I can tell he's unconvinced, too. He doesn't know what's going on.

He shakes his head. 'I'm sure we're just running some kind of operations test or—'

A low steady drone screeches across the air.

Jenkins gasps. 'It's the siren!'

The doctor's eyes bulge. 'It can't be.'

They scurry, knocking over a table in their haste, sending tools clattering, and leaving me strapped to the gurney. Anxious voices fade away, collide with others in the hallway, and then I'm all alone, stuck to a table, unable to even turn my head.

Great.

Soon I can't even hear voices in the distance. Just the siren. An automated voice fills the air, speaking over the unremitting wail. *All personnel evacuate through the stair-well. Proceed with caution.*

I surge against my bindings. Hopeless. My gaze fixes on the glass room where my audience once stood. Empty now. Several of the chairs are toppled over; the door of that room yawns open. Tantalizingly close, and yet I can't get there.

Over the siren's wail, I hear a sound. I strain to listen, thinking it's running feet. The swinging door behind me gives the slightest thump—like a hand pushing against it— and then a faint creak of hinges.

Someone's entered the room. I hold my breath, almost afraid to hope . . .

'Jacinda?'

Even as I recognize Will's voice I hear the fear, and re-alize he can't see my face. I'm lying as silent as stone. He probably thinks I'm dead. I moan against the tape covering my mouth and squirm my body to let him know I'm alive.

45

Then he's in front of me, Cassian and Tamra right behind him. Only my sister is manifested. Not Cassian.

I surrender to my relief—and get a hot surge of Cassian's relief, too. Coupled with my own, the emotion overwhelms me and I sink deeper onto the gurney.

'Jacinda!' Will's there, surrounding me with his warmth. It hasn't been that long, but it's like seeing him with fresh eyes, devouring the sight of him with a hunger I've never felt before. Not until I was lowered into this abyss.

As Cassian and Tamra work at the rest of my straps, he tears the tape from my mouth. I hiss involuntarily at the pain, but it doesn't really bother me. I'm free. I'll never look at anything the same again, never take anything or anyone for granted.

Will winces and brushes his thumb over my raw mouth, pressing a quick feverish kiss to my lips. He clasps my face in both of his hands, his eyes searching and hungry at the same time. His bright gaze lands on my bloodied strands of hair and he peers closer at the wound there. 'What did they do to you? Are you all right? '

'It's not that deep. I'm fine,' I say, knowing, of course, he can't understand me. I'm speaking draki.

'She's fine,' Cassian answers, his dark visage glowering in the crimson light as he sweeps me with his purply dark gaze. 'Quick. See if she can stand.'

Will's eyes flash, revealing only a flicker of irritation at Cassian's tone. Ever the prince.

Will's hands move fast, unbolting the last strap, and in seconds I'm free, sliding off the gurney into Will's arms.

Then I'm in Tamra's arms, wrenched into her embrace with more strength than I realized she possessed. She steps back to look me over. 'This has had to be the worst day of my life.'

I almost smile, thinking it probably doesn't compare to mine.

Cassian studies me but doesn't move to hug me. His face is a stiff mask. It reminds me of everything that's happened before this moment. Even though we came here together to rescue Miram, even though we're bonded and as close as two draki can be, emotionally linked, we're not . . . *together*.

Not the way he would have us be.

As I stare at him, it all washes over me again. That I've chosen Will. Instead of him. Instead of the pride.

Cassian looks from me to Will and back again, and his irritation crawls over my skin like a living thing. His dark gaze flashes purple, vertical pupils quivering. He blinks and the annoyance fades from his eyes, but I still feel it lingering in him. In me.

'Where's Miram?' he asks, all business now.

I nod once, refocusing. 'Follow me.'

We rush through the swinging doors, but I stop as I confront Tamra's handiwork. Her mist lingers, drifting over the bodies of fallen enkros. Maybe only half a dozen litter the floor. The ones that didn't make it out.

At my glance, she shrugs, the tips of her shimmering wings bouncing up over her shoulders. I push on, stepping around the bodies, leading them down corridors to the tune of the incessant alarm and automated voice advising all personnel to proceed with caution.

My ears prick, detecting running feet in the distance. Apparently Tamra's sleep-inducing mist didn't infiltrate every corner of the facility.

47

The echo of steps fades off the hollow space of the corridors, and I guess that it's the last of the enkros fleeing.

We don't see anyone else about, and I'm hoping, fervently, that all the draki are still inside their cells and haven't been moved in the mass exodus. The enkros didn't pause to bother with me, after all.

Relief rolls through me when we reach the prison block. They're still there. Some standing, some pacing the small cells, all clearly freaked out from the alarm. They watch us with wary eyes as we enter the room.

Cassian sprints ahead to the front of Miram's cell. He touches the Plexiglas, presses one large hand to the barrier as if he can reach her.

I run to the observation table and study the panel with all its monitors and gadgets, trying to figure out how to open the cells.

Tamra walks slowly up and down the row of cells, examining all the other draki. She stops before the cell with Lia. It's my first good look at her, too. She's just a girl—the smallest draki I've ever seen—and I know Tamra is taken aback to see one so young here.

'Jacinda, I think I got it.' Will's voice draws my attention. He points to a row of switches, each one numbered. He flips number three. The cell Cassian stands in front of slides open.

Miram steps out and falls into Cassian's arms, sobbing. I smile, lightness spreading through me as I watch Cassian lift her off the ground in a hug. Cassian's happiness trips through me. It's impossible not to absorb his absolute joy at finding her alive.

'Jacinda.'

I look up at Tamra. She's turned towards me, but motioning to Lia's cell over her shoulder. The message in her frosty eyes is clear. She wants to free the girl.

I'll do more than that. With a nod, I use both hands to flip up every switch all at once. All the cells slide open.

They don't wait for an invitation. Draki dive out simultaneously. Several fly past us without a word, intent only on escape. The one I assume is Roc, an onyx, winks and nods his thanks as he wings past us.

Lia lingers, her large blue eyes staring from me and Tamra and back again, uncertain.

I move away from the panel and approach her. 'C'mon. You should stick with us.' I didn't realize I was going to say that until it falls from my lips, but it's so obvious to me. Of course I'm not leaving her alone.

Suddenly the automated voice changes its tune, becomes a new mantra.

Warning. Retreat to stairwell immediately. Operation Lilith will commence in five minutes.

Operation Lilith? The enkros must have safely evacuated and moved into plan B. Whatever that is, it can't be good for us.

'I think it's time we get out of here,' Will announces.

I nod and we all rush for the doors, ready to head for the stairwell since there's obviously a reason no one is using the elevators. Even if they work, it's probably not a great idea in an emergency. If the power went off, we would be stuck inside.

'Wait!'

We pause, watching as Lia hurries back to the control frame. She glances at the open cells for a long moment before considering the panel of buttons.

'Come on!' I call, thinking those five minutes are fading away quickly.

With a firm nod, as though reaching a decision, she hits a switch.

The back wall of the cells slide open, exposing the lush green of the simulated forest.

I rush forward. 'What are you doing?'

She grabs my wrist, stopping me from hitting the switch again to close that wall—to shield us from that world . . . *from him.*

'We can't leave him in there,' she says solemnly. Her big eyes, so like Az's, peer up at me, *into* me, seeming to know just what to say to affect me.

'He'll kill us.' Even as I utter this, I'm not totally sure. If he's free, I doubt he'll care enough to come after us.

She shakes her head. 'I don't think so. He'll focus on escaping, just like us.'

I angle my head, studying her. For one so young, she's wise.

'He's crazy,' Miram whispers fervently to Cassian.

'What's she talking about?' Cassian demands.

'There's another draki in there . . .' My voice stops. I stare into Lia's eyes, the vertical pupils shuddering with intensity. She's determined to help the grey one . . . and I don't really disagree with her.

He doesn't deserve to be a captive any more than any other draki. Any more than I do.

I glance back into the pulsing world of green, so at odds with the rest of this sterile, cold underworld.

'Jacinda.' Will tugs my arm. 'We have to go.'

'Fine,' I say, 'let's just get out of here before he realizes the doors are open.'

We flee the room. No one asks for further explanation, and I guess everyone is just satisfied that we're finally on our way out. I slide Cassian a glance. He runs with one hand wrapped around Miram's arm, as if he's somehow afraid he might lose her again.

Then an awful screech tears through the air. It's a sound I recognize. Was it only hours ago that I heard that sound, convinced I might die?

The grey one is free.

'This way!' Will shouts without having to be told that the unnatural sound comes from a creature we do not want to face.

We run down another corridor, feet and shoes slapping hard on the tile. I glance at Tamra. Her white hair looks red in the glow of emergency lights suffusing the air. The way it used to look. The way I look.

Ahead there's an open threshold and just beyond it a set of wide concrete steps.

'The stairwell,' Tamra shouts, a smile splitting her face. The first one I've seen from her since I persuaded her to join us on this journey.

I smile, too. We're almost there. We've made it.

Then the alarm cuts off, along with the automated voice blaring from above. An eerie silence descends—the only sound that of our crashing breaths as we near that first bottom step. The first step to our freedom.

The sudden plunge into quiet forces us into slow motion, makes us all pause. I hesitate, looking around uncertainly.

A mistake. Suddenly a large steel door slides shut before us, walling off the stairwell.

And sealing us in.

51

CHAPTER SIX

I t seems that no one says anything for quite some time, but it can't be more than thirty seconds. We just stare in a sort of stunned disbelief at the spot where there once were stairs. Stairs that are supposed to lead us out of here.

'Where's the elevator?' Tamra blurts, spinning around, her gaze searching as if she's going to suddenly find it right behind us.

It's the only reminder we need. There's another way out of here. Risk or no risk, climbing into an elevator is our only chance.

We hurry down the wide halls, our shadows dark and fluid shapes on the red-tinged walls. Draki and human—the combination strikes a chill to my heart, especially in this environment where draki and human don't blend.

And then I feel guilty, because I know what I am. I know what Will's not. And I already decided it didn't matter. I believe that.

I shake my head and concentrate on the path before me, the steady pound of my feet, ignoring the whisper in the back of my head. The voice that reminds me those five minutes are almost up.

We pull to a stop at the elevator. The doors are shut, the silver panels sealed tight. Will pushes the button, hitting hard two times. Nothing. No light. No sign that it's working at all.

'They've locked the place down,' Cassian announces grimly.

'What do you mean? What are you saying?' Tamra looks wildly at each of us. 'We can't get out? Like . . . ever?'

'It must be procedure to shut everything down when something goes wrong—like us infiltrating,' Will explains. Even without understanding Tamra, he can guess the gist of our conversation.

'So we're stuck?' I ask, shaking my head, refusing to believe that. 'For how long?'

'They don't want to risk any of us escaping,' Lia announces.

I growl with disgust. We shouldn't have gone back for the grey one. We would have made it out of here like the other draki, all of whom are probably flying home right now. If we had just kept going, we'd be free. But now we're stuck down here. With *him*.

The flesh at the back of my neck prickles and I shiver, glancing around as though he were there. Ready to pick up where we left off. It's all in my head. There's nothing behind us but a hazy red-infused hall. When I turn back, my gaze finds Lia.

She gives a small shrug of apology, reading my mind

perfectly. *Yeah*. Now she wishes she hadn't pushed that button to free him.

I open my mouth, deciding I better warn the others exactly what we're up against—that there's a seven-foot grey draki capable of butchering someone with a single touch. That a brush against him can sever a limb.

Only a new danger appears first.

The thin tubing running along the edges of the ceiling comes to life and spurts out a cloudy mist with a faint hissing sound—like the starting of a sprinkler.

Will points, his voice hard: 'They're gassing the facility!'

'With what?' I growl, even though he can't understand me. My thoughts lurch as I stare at that growing fog. I don't think the enkros will kill us—not when we're valuable to them alive.

Cassian shakes his head, squinting at the faint spray. 'I don't know . . . maybe it's something to knock us unconscious.'

I nod. That makes more sense than their gassing us to death and killing every draki captive. They'd lose their entire collection before getting to fully conduct their experiments.

Tamra attacks the elevator's lightless button as if it might somehow start working. 'Whatever they're trying to do, we're pretty much screwed if we don't get out of here!'

Lia hugs herself and falls back against a wall as if her legs suddenly can't support her weight. 'I'm sorry. We're not going to escape, are we?' she whispers, shaking her head and sending her blue-streaked dark hair tossing around her small shoulders.

And the sight of this small, helpless girl does something to me.

She shouldn't be here. None of us should.

Something twists and squeezes tightly inside me. I press four fingers to the centre of my chest but it doesn't help. The pain doesn't go away and I inhale deeply—then stop abruptly, catching myself. I glare at the fumes circling high above us. Eventually those fumes will make their way down to us, eat through us—and do whatever it is they are supposed to do. A sudden calmness comes over me. I drop my hand from my chest and look from my sister to Cassian and then Will, realizing this might be it. *And if it is, I know whose arms I need to feel around me as I draw my final breath.*

Will looks at me then, as if reading my mind. He holds my stare for several moments before looking away again, back to the tubing spitting out its fumes. I shudder at the thought of what they will do with him when they find him in here with us. If they discover that he's not really like them—not quite human, not quite draki—but something in between . . .

The idea of that physically pains me. I suck in a deep breath. I may feel Cassian, but I want Will.

I step towards Will. He's still busy studying the piping, determined to figure out a way to save us, doubtlessly contemplating a way to stop the gas from wreaking its damage. But there's no way. Time is fading and I won't have my last moments wasted.

I touch his face, my fingers firm on his jaw, angling him to look back down at me. We don't have words right now. I can't demanifest. I need to stay at my strongest. And I'm strongest as a draki. But I'll have him see me, hear me in his heart.

His eyes are intent and worried, bright with a fever to do something, to save us. *Me*. I know he's more worried for me right now than for himself. Because that's so like him. So Will. Good, caring, self-sacrificing. It makes me feel all the worse for dragging him into this—into my world.

I smile at him and brush my thumb across his lips. Something flickers in his hazel eyes, understanding. His head swoops down and he kisses me swiftly.

I tell myself if this is how it all ends, it's not such a bad way to go. I slide my fingers around his neck, caress the soft skin there, so much cooler than my own, and don't care that we have an audience. I tune them out, focus only on Will. On this. I won't let any of the other stuff take this from me.

His lips are cool, too. Dry and chilly as they move against mine. That doesn't faze me—not the differences, what I am, what he is, what we aren't—none of that matters any more.

Frustration wells up inside me, irritation . . . and a vague ache starts humming inside my chest. I try to focus on Will, on the taste of him. It's never been a hard task before. I try, but that vague ache grows, becomes sharper, more acute. I pull back, rubbing my fingers at the centre of my chest again.

'What is it?' he asks in concern.

I shake my head, feeling dazed. I gasp. *Pain*. The discomfort coincides with a sudden banging. I blink against the world of red, looking around, spotting Cassian a few feet away, now fully manifested.

He's pounding his fists into the wall until his knuckles gleam wet with purply blood. I wince, cringing as the cement buckles and cracks beneath the pressure, chunks falling to his feet. I've always known he was strong. Onyx typically are. My father was.

But seeing Cassian like this, *feeling* this . . .

I curl and uncurl my hands, the echo of his pain vibrating in my bones. His anger reaches me, toxic as venom. For a heartbeat I worry it's fuelled by me and Will . . . watching us kiss. I've made my choice, but still, that doesn't mean I want to hurt Cassian. Especially in this, possibly our last moment. I don't want to cause him pain.

I probe deeper, feel him there inside me . . . reaching for whatever it is driving him to act so crazy. Did he just snap? Miram shouts his name, wringing her hands. Fear is all over her face, and I'm quite certain she's never seen her brother so out of control before. Cassian has always been the steady one, calm and strong.

Then I realize his only thought is wrapped up in survival, in breaking free.

I watch as he attacks the wall, his muscles straining as he works, hints of dark charcoal rippling beneath the surface of his flesh like winks of dark night.

He punches and tears at the cement in a frenzy. As foolish as this method might be, he doesn't care. His desperation seeps into me and I slide forward half a step . . . as if I am about to join him in his madness.

I stop, shake my head. This is where it gets confusing. Separating his feelings from mine.

'What are you doing?' I shout. 'You can't break through the wall. We're underground!'

I move to approach him, but Will clamps on my arm, holding me back. He's probably afraid I'll get caught in one of Cassian's savage swings.

I wave an arm. 'What are you going to do? Tunnel through the ground?'

He sends me a quick glare and continues hitting the wall. Dirt and bits of loose rock fly. A sharp pebble hits me in the cheek. I press my hand to the spot. The cement starts to give way to hard-packed earth, a dark brown soil that smells loamy and rich.

'That sounds just about right,' he snaps as he continues his attack.

And then I realize he's serious.

The spraying mist starts to descend closer to us now.

Sporadic coughs hiccup through our group. I wave at the air before my nose as if that will disperse whatever effect the fumes wield.

'Can we do that?' Tamra asks. She squeezes her hands anxiously in front of her as if praying this might be a true possibility.

'If anyone can break us out of here, Cassian can,' Miram supplies, her fear gone now, replaced with total confidence that her older brother can solve anything. I roll my eyes and resist snapping that even Cassian can't claw a path to freedom. We're buried too deeply underground.

'I can do it,' Will says in a low voice, watching us all intently, absorbing our exchange even without understanding everything. Then he announces again, 'I can do it.'

At his vehemence, Cassian hesitates. He pulls back his fist, blood dripping thickly from his shattered knuckles to the tiled floor.

'Will,' I murmur, and even though the sound of his name on my lips is different, more a growl than actual speech, he turns his head to stare at me. One look in his hazel eyes and I know. I understand what he means. I see him again as I saw him fighting with Corbin, earth shifting and flying at his command.

'Stand back,' Will commands.

Surprisingly, Cassian does.

We all watch, trying to keep our breaths small and sparse, as if we can somehow *not* inhale the air that's becoming more and more tainted.

Will faces off in front of the busted wall. Miram starts hacking, covering her mouth with both hands. Soon, Lia joins in. The sounds of their coughs only make everything more tense, more urgent. I wince in sympathy as Cassian folds Miram into his arms. What if we were wrong? What if this gas is meant to kill us?

With both hands poised in the air in front of him, Will focuses on the wall. I stare at his wide flat palms, willing them to do something, to possess the same power I'd observed before when he took on Corbin. His hands start to tremble, but nothing. The gouged wall doesn't show any sign of movement.

Cassian grunts with disgust.

I shake my head. I don't know what I'd been expecting. To see something miraculous? That he could perhaps do something more? Something even the earth draki of my pride couldn't do? Ridiculous. This isn't like my dream where he can sprout wings and take to the skies with me.

Then suddenly there's a thundering crash. A huge cloud of smoke billows into the hall, temporarily blinding me. For a moment, I think it's a sudden influx of gas shooting from the tubing above us. No more slow and lingering death.

But then I realize it's not just smoke everywhere. It's debris too. Particles and bits of wall cover every inch of my skin and sting my eyes.

I look back to the wall and gasp to see that not only is it gone . . . but a crude hole several feet deep takes its place.

Will did it. He'd actually manipulated earth to create a way out. Of course, he needs to do it several more times for us to actually escape.

'How did you know . . .?' My voice fades in wonder. And of course, what would be the point in asking? He can't understand me.

Will meets my bewildered gaze. He must read the question there because he shrugs. 'I don't know. I just knew I could do it. A feeling . . . impulse came over me.'

'Nice job,' Tamra says approvingly, stepping inside the ragged hole that Will just created. 'Can you do it some more?' She gestures forward.

The rest of us follow, stepping into the fissure in the wall one by one . . . but something gives me pause. The prickly feeling at the back of my neck is back. The tiny hairs there tingle and vibrate. I turn and look out at the corridor.

Behind me I hear the others urging Will for a repeat, to do it again and tunnel us an escape path out of here. But not every voice is there. Cassian's isn't.

Will obliges, and another boom shakes the air, radiating from the ground and up my legs. A giant wave of wind, dust, and debris hits me in the back. I stagger for a moment before catching my balance.

Still, I stare out at the corridor from where we made our escape and find Cassian standing amid the possibly toxic spray, looking off to his right, his attention fixed on something. He coughs, covering his mouth with his hand. He needs to get out of there, but he's lingering for some reason.

'Cassian? What is it?'

He shakes his head. 'I don't know. Something—'

He doesn't finish the rest of his sentence. Suddenly he's gone, ripped out of my sight by a streak of grey.

The one we let loose.

'Cassian!' I scream, plunging after him, knowing what I'm about to face . . . and knowing that this time there won't be any enkros to tear us apart.

CHAPTER SEVEN

I dive from the crater back into the poisonous corridor. 'Jacinda!' Will's there, grabbing my hand, stopping me from going any farther. His expression is earnest and desperate, willing me to stop, stay. Stay with him. It's all I've ever wanted. But I can't. Not now.

'We have to help Cassian,' I rattle off in draki tongue. Will pulls my hand harder to follow him back inside the tunnel.

I shake my head with a growl, remembering he can't understand. And yet I can't leave Cassian. I can't abandon him. Even now, in the space of the heartbeat that I look back at the others, I feel the deep pain radiating through Cassian's body. It almost bends me over at the waist.

I inhale a hissing breath and force myself to move through it, reminding myself that it's not real for me. It's not *my* pain. It's his. And I have to end it.

I yank my hand free from Will and charge down the hall to a T-junction. I look left and right—spot Cassian tangled at the end of the corridor with the grey draki.

They're a blur, moving much too fast; I can already smell the blood on the air. I don't need to see his wounds to know that it's Cassian's blood I scent.

I take off toward them, half running, half flying. Grey on black, they fight, tangle with each other wildly. It's hard to distinguish between the two of them. I cry out as a spurt of blood arches across the air, narrowly missing me.

I have to stop it. I can't let this go on. There won't be anything of Cassian left.

I focus my attention on the largest area of grey I can detect and release a gust of fire, desperately hoping my aim is accurate.

I make contact. The draki roars and tears free from Cassian. I focus on the grey one, fire dancing on my tongue, preparing to let loose another blast of heat on him.

His knifelike scales shake and make a strange whistling sound. The protruding scales on his shoulder retract and flatten. His fingers tenderly test the charred flesh of his shoulder, growling as the flesh slides and slips between his fingers like melted wax.

The sight of this—of what I can do, the damage I can bring to my own kind—makes my stomach twist sickly.

'Jacinda!' Will arrives breathlessly at my side, coughing from the increasingly smoky air. His stare swings to the grey draki and he lets loose a curse.

The grey one drops his hand from his shoulder and squares off.

'He looks pissed. You do that to him?' Wills asks amid a coughing fit.

I nod. 'Uh-huh.' I draw a deep breath, ready to pull the heat up from my lungs, but my airway feels too thin, constricted. I inhale and then gasp, choking and hacking violently as I draw in a lungful of toxic fumes.

Will understands instantly. I have no defence. No fire. I need good, clean oxygen. His hand grabs mine. 'We have to go now!'

He's right, of course. We have to go before the fumes knock us out . . . or worse.

But not without Cassian.

I lock eyes with Cassian, stepping forward, not thinking. Not thinking that I still have to get around the grey draki to get to him.

Cassian shakes his head, eyes glinting fiercely at me. 'Go, get out of here!'

He can't mean for us to leave him.

'Cassian, no!' I surge forward another step with a flap of wings, ready for another go, even if I can't breathe fire. Will clamps down on my shoulder, yanking me back.

The grey draki's legs brace wide, ready for me. The pupils of his pewter eyes shudder. I look again at Cassian, beyond my reach.

'Go,' he shouts again from around the draki's legs, his voice breaking into a savage spasm of coughing. His gaze flicks to Will. 'Get her out of here!'

Somehow, intuitively, Will understands him. Or maybe it's just the obvious thing to do. Only not to me.

Will wraps an arm around my waist, dragging me back.

'Cassian,' I scream.

Will moves his other arm in a wide arc and then pushes his palm out in what's becoming a familiar gesture.

The earth falls before my eyes in a roar of dirt and debris.

'Get back,' Will yells behind us to the others. His grip on me tightens as he jerks me back into the tunnel. We land in a tangled pile.

Then Will's on his feet, hauling me back as the curtain of dirt keeps coming at us in a ravenous tidal wave. But I don't care. Coughing violently, I jerk free and jump to my feet.

I charge into the maelstrom of raining earth. 'Cassian!' I'm not the only one screaming. Miram is there, too, calling for her brother. In this, our desperation to save him, we're unified.

'Jacinda, no!' Will grabs me again. 'It's too late! We have to go!'

I spin around and yank my arm free of him. 'What have you done?'

He doesn't understand my words. But he doesn't need to. He knows.

His eyes harden. 'We have to keep moving. We'll run out of oxygen soon down here.' Turning, he strides past the others. Leaves me to do what he must.

Miram sobs near my feet, beating at the wall of dirt where the opening to the hallway used to be. I close a hand around her arm and pull her to her feet. For once, she lets me help her. She feels slighter, thinner than I remember. Captivity will do that, I guess. My heart twists as I recall the time she endured as a prisoner. And now this. Losing Cassian. It wasn't supposed to be like this. I'd never imagined anything as terrible as this. My hand strokes her arm. We all move, following Will.

'I'm sorry,' Lia says in a whisper, squeezing beside me in the narrow space. 'I shouldn't have freed him. I just couldn't stand the thought—'

I wave a hand, silencing her. It's not her fault. I could have stopped her. I let sympathy get in the way. I won't be so stupid again.

'Jacinda?' Tamra looks searchingly at me and then back behind us. 'Cassian?'

'We can't save him,' I bite out, then flinch as Miram starts weeping again.

I look behind us again to where the dirt still swirls in the air. I see the disbelief on her face. She's torn, trying to wrap her head around what I already know. Cassian is lost to us.

I open my mouth to tell her that there's nothing to be done, when sudden burning pain lances me, nearly bringing me to my knees. I release Miram and crash against the rough rock wall with a gasp.

Tamra reaches for me. 'Jacinda? What is it?'

Cassian. It's Cassian.

Miram watches me wide-eyed, her terror as palpable as the dirt particles swimming around us, and I clamp my lips together as my chest explodes in fiery hot pain that rivals the ache in my heart.

'Jace, what is it?' Worry etches itself in the smooth lines of Tamra's face.

I shake my head and swallow back a scream of agony. I'm not about to tell her what I know—that Cassian is being hurt, tortured somewhere by a devil draki. That I feel it happening.

Even as much as she dislikes Cassian, there's still a history there that she can't escape. A history of caring and longing, of wanting him and never getting him. She wouldn't want him hurt, wouldn't want him . . . *dead*. Nor do I want to tell Miram what's happening and risk her refusing to escape with us. Cassian would want me to see his sister to safety. I can't let this have all been for nothing.

I force myself to move, trying to pretend I can't feel the pain, that I'm not leaving a piece of myself behind. 'I'm OK. Let's go.'

Will works ahead of us, using his newfound powers to stretch out our tunnel and lead us to freedom. We fight the swirl of dust and earth and follow several paces in his wake.

I stare at Will's back, trying not to blame him. Trying not to be angry. It's a hard battle. After several minutes, I sense that he's tiring, but he doesn't stop. Doesn't quit. It's not in him to quit. I know that best of all. He keeps going, pushing ahead, dirt and earth spitting all around us in a rushing roar. I think of asking him if he knows where he's going—are we going to emerge smack in the middle of town? That would be awkward.

I almost laugh at the image. But I don't. It could happen. And we could still not make it out of this. Still *die*. Even if Will doesn't know where we're going he can't stop now. There's no going back. Behind us death waits. So I say nothing and trust him, letting him lead us out of this hell.

CHAPTER EIGHT

I'm not sure how long we travel underground. Time is suspended. It feels as though we're trapped in the very belly of the earth. Will begins to slow. My eyes have become long accustomed to the darkness, but I still squint at him through the gritty haze of dust as he motions for me to stop.

'Wait here. I'll be right back.'

I halt, waving an arm out at my side to keep the others from continuing. Will moves ahead, curving slightly until I lose sight of him in the billowing cloud of dirt.

Then it's just us girls in the dark. I feel the breath of them around me, moist and rasping in the crackling dry air, earth particles floating like fairy dust all around us. I jump when I finally hear the sound of Will's voice.

'C'mon! It's clear!'

We eagerly move ahead, following the path he's carved for us. I'm leading over the uneven ground and the first to see the light ahead. It's like waking to sunlight. I blink and squint, shading my eyes with my hand. Through the press of ragged earth around us, I make out a jagged opening in the distance. Bits of roots and grass dangle around its edge.

I don't see Will at all. He's gone, and for a moment my chest feels tight, my heart fluttering with panic. Then his face is there, popping back inside through the opening that's scarcely big enough to fit his shoulders. 'It's all clear. We're not far from where we left the van.' He tosses some clothes at us. 'Demanifest and get dressed.'

We comply. Miram, Tamra, and I slip on our clothes. I pass a sweatshirt and trousers to Lia, pausing as I see her as a human for the first time. Enormous eyes, freckles, and a nose that upturns ever so slightly. She scarcely looks twelve. The apology is still there in her eyes, and I wish I could take her guilt away from her. She's too young to feel such heavy responsibility. The burden of who lives and dies in an enkros cesspit shouldn't be hers.

'Let's go.' The three girls follow me as I squeeze to the surface. I squint like a mole emerging from its hole. The last of the day's sunlight is fading, infusing the air with a red-gold hue. Motes dance on the fading beams. I drop on the ground, allowing my fingers to curl into the earth. I inhale a ragged breath of sweet, fresh air. Cassian. The thought of him, left behind, tears through me like a freshly opened wound.

I reach for Cassian inside myself, hoping to find him there, hoping he can sense me. *Your sister is safe, Cassian. She's OK. I'm OK.*

I *will* him to know this, hoping to reassure him. Hoping to give him a reason to fight . . . to find a way back to us.

Then I feel him. Like a faint cry in the night, his relief comes to me, wraps around me like a warm wind.

'Jacinda.'

I glance up. Will stands at the back of the van, holding one door open and waving us over. His anxious expression reminds me we're not out of this yet. I rise to my feet, reluctant to go even as I know we must. Leaving, somehow, feels like shutting the door forever on Cassian. Now I feel him, but I know from Mum that the more distance between us, the weaker our connection grows, and this makes my chest tighten with unease. Right now, the only thing I have left of him is our bond.

Will watches me, his gaze intent, and I know he guesses my thoughts. I feel guilty. And then annoyed. I hate that I can't openly be broken up about leaving Cassian without worrying how that makes Will feel.

Tamra helps Miram to the van. I watch the girl as she clambers inside, reminded of an old woman.

Lia glances from Will to me, clearly hesitant, and I guess she senses the tension. Her gaze lingers on Will and I know she's trying to figure him out—this non-draki with the draki talent to manipulate the earth.

'It's all right. Get inside,' I say.

Then it's just Will and me outside the van . . . and nothing feels 'all right'.

I might have demanifested, but I still simmer beneath my skin. Cassian's emotions ripple through me as I face Will. Even distracted with this, I want to rail and weep and strike Will for what he did. Sentiments all unfair, I know, but I'm the one standing here *feeling* every bit of Cassian's suffering. I'm living it alongside of him.

'Get in,' he says, reminding me that whatever I have to say, now isn't the time. We're standing barely outside the enkros stronghold with the enkros running loose. We're not safe yet.

I move towards the back of the van just as a helicopter rips through the air above us, flying so low it creates a strong wind. Then two more roar past. *Reinforcements.*

I stare up at the sky and then look away, glance down the hillside, spotting several vehicles driving at high speed along the main road leading up to the stronghold's gates. In the fading light, I can see the flurry of activity in its parking lot.

'Now! Let's go,' Will shouts.

I dive into the back of the van.

In seconds, I hear the driver's door slam shut and we're moving, engine revving. The van turns sharply, tossing us around in the back. Lia slides into me. I wrap an arm around the girl and steady her as the van rumbles all around us like a purring beast.

Tamra holds Miram, whose gaze drills into me. 'What about my brother?' For her, he's not lost. Tamra attempts to shush her, but Miram will have none of it. 'Jacinda?' she demands.

I shake my head, unable to say anything.

'Are we just leaving him?' she presses. 'Forgetting about him?'

'He's gone,' Lia whispers.

Miram's attention swerves to the girl. '*You!* Shut up! You made us set that monster loose. This is your fault.'

Lia shudders in my arms and turns her face away, staring stoically at the doors.

'Jacinda?' Tamra slides down beside me and lightly touches my shoulder. Even though it's Tamra, I jerk from the contact.

71

Cassian's terror is all around me now, cloying and deep; it sinks into my pores and roots in my bones. It's all I can feel, all I am—a creature that lives and breathes fear.

I press close to the cold metal of the van wall. Still hugging myself, I shake, fight the onslaught of Cassian's emotions.

The most basic part of me longs to break free, but the rest of me clings to Cassian, struggling to keep our connection as the distance between us grows. He's not lost as long as I *feel* him.

'Jacinda?' Tamra repeats my name again, insistent for some kind of acknowledgment.

'I'm fine. Just don't . . . touch me,' I say through gritted teeth as the sound of another helicopter roars nearby.

Locked in the shadows of the van, all our gazes swing upward, worried the helicopter will spot us. We release a collective breath as the sound of whirring blades recedes.

Cassian's agony intensifies then, the fear so bitter it floods my mouth and drops me to my side. I can't care or think about anything else but this. An icy burn penetrates my body. I hiss. Arch my spine. Releasing Lia, I thrust my fists down hard, grinding my knuckles into the unforgiving floor, as if that pressure could offer me some relief.

'Jacinda? What's wrong?' Tamra cries, her voice a distant echo in my ears.

Another chopper flies overhead, deafeningly loud and then gone, a faint drone as it fades away.

'Cassian,' I get out from between clenched teeth.

It's not the grey draki doing this to him. I know this with a deep vibration in my bones.

Something else has him . . . is with him. His fear tastes different . . . more acrid.

I close my eyes as my agony—his agony—swings into something else.

Dread sweeps over me. I curl into a small, self-contained ball, holding myself tightly.

And suddenly I'm fine. I'm fine. But *he* isn't. Cassian isn't fine. He isn't anything. He's gone. Just like that.

Like a string snapped. There's nothing there anymore. No connection. No bond. *No Cassian.* It's too soon for distance to have severed us. The sound of my racing heart fills my ears. I poke around inside myself, hunting for him, some proof that he's still there. With me. But nothing.

No Cassian.

I lurch up with a gasp and scream his name. 'Cassian!'

We pull over hours later.

I've stopped screaming, aware that I was freaking out the others. I can't imagine what Will must have thought stuck behind the wheel, driving to the sound of me in the back. Now I'm just hugging myself again, rocking and swaying as if I were a child in need of comfort. And I am. In so many ways. From the beginning, Cassian has always been there. Even in Chaparral when he wasn't there, he was there, a constant spectre. And then he did appear—never going away even when I wanted him to. Always looking out for me. And now he's gone.

Tamra tries to comfort me, but I can hardly speak to the others. Especially Miram. How can I look at her and tell her what I know for a certainty? That Cassian is gone. Dead.

At one point, Tamra whispers to her, explaining how Cassian and I were forced into bonding back in the pride— and that I still chose Will.

I see Miram pull back, the fury flashing in the dull brown of her eyes. She turns to me with a look I know well. She loathes me now more than ever. In her eyes, I've rejected everything I should have embraced—our pride, the draki way. Her brother. She can't understand this, and I don't expect her to.

How could I choose Will over the precious draki *prince* of our pride? It's the question I see in her face, and there's no simple reason I can give.

Then again, there's nothing simple about Will. I think back to what he can do—bend earth, resist shading, his immense strength—and it's glaringly inaccurate to consider him a human. But then I can't think of him as a draki either. And this strikes me as sad. Will doesn't belong anywhere. Not among humans. Not among draki.

But he belongs with me. The conviction is still there, as senseless and dangerous as always, seeping into my bones, my heart. A fact I wouldn't change even if I could.

The back door of the van swings open, and Will stands there in the quiet twilight. Dark woods crouch at his back and I know he's made certain we're far from the stronghold. Wherever we are, we're safe for now.

His gaze sweeps all of us before settling on me. The concern is there, shimmering in the hazel depths of his eyes. He undoubtedly heard my screams, but couldn't stop until now.

'Are you OK?' Will asks.

I hold his gaze. 'He's gone. Cassian's dead.' My voice chokes on the words, hating to say them. Especially in front of Tamra and Miram, but I can't hide my knowledge from them forever.

Will is silent. His face reveals nothing. I catch a glimmer of something more in his eyes, but I'm not sure what it means.

Miram lets out a wail and falls into Tamra's arms.

'I'm sorry,' he finally says.

I feel my face threaten to crumple and draw a deep breath, fighting back the burn of fresh tears. I don't need another meltdown. But it's horrible. Feeling this grief over Cassian, but unable to show it because I don't want to be insensitive to Will—don't want him to think I was in love with Cassian.

A moment of awkward silence passes, and he looks around us. 'We need to drive a little more. I'm not comfortable stopping yet, but I wanted to check in on you all. A few more hours and we can eat and get some rest.'

He waits for a moment as if I'm going to respond to this. None of us speaks. The only sounds are Miram's sobs. I don't look at him again. I can't. Not with these horrible feelings churning inside me. Instead, I give a sharp nod.

The doors slam shut. I listen to the crunch of his footsteps and the thud of the driver's door. In moments, the van is rumbling all around us again and we're moving on into the night.

'You did this, Jacinda,' Miram whispers heatedly, ignoring my sister shushing her. 'You did this. Cassian is dead because of you.'

'And you had no part?' I bite out, hurting so much inside, and unwilling to endure all the pain for this— all the blame. 'Weren't you the one who followed me and got us caught? Weren't you the one who refused to escape with me when we first had a chance?'

She glares at me hatefully, and this almost makes her bland visiocrypter eyes look alive. Something else shines there, too—the awareness that I'm right. She can't hide her guilt completely. And then I remember Cassian, and the love he felt for her. Knowing Miram will forever blame herself makes me feel worse. Even Tamra looks at me with such disappointment, and I feel awful.

Miram swipes at her nose with a sniff and fixes her gaze on the wall of the van.

Lia blows out a breath. 'And I thought I had it bad with all the drama in my life.'

I look at Lia, this girl, this stranger. I don't possess the energy to ask her about her life and where she comes from and what her drama could possibly be. Any other time I would have loved to meet a draki from another pride—to compare notes and find out if there was a better way of life outside my pride, away from Severin's autocratic ways. But I can't think about that now. Maybe later.

I lie on my side, slide my hand beneath my cheek, and stare blindly. Strange, I've left the enkros stronghold behind, the prison that almost broke me down, but I don't feel as though I've escaped.

I still feel beaten, forever their prisoner.

CHAPTER NINE

We stop several hours later, pulling to the side of a small rural road. We need to discuss our next steps. The plan was to split up at this point—Cassian and Miram returning to the pride while we go our own way. Clearly that's changed now.

I can't envision strolling back into the township. Especially now. Without Cassian. And yet Miram still needs to get home.

I swallow and close my eyes. A target will forever mark my back after the pride learns what happened to Cassian. Lifting my face to the night, I let a breeze caress my skin and know that they will never let me go, never stop hunting me. They'll blame me for Cassian. Severin will never rest until I pay, until I'm back with the pride, a prisoner. He'll send one of his strongest after me. *Corbin.* He might be Cassian's cousin, but he doesn't possess one ounce of his integrity. He'd show me no mercy.

'Jacinda.'

I jerk at the sound of my name. I'm the only one still inside the vehicle. Tamra stands outside the van, looking in at me, her expression tight with worry, her smooth brow wrinkled. Will is just beyond her, shifting his weight on both feet. I've never seen him like this—so uncertain at how to approach me.

Scooting out, I drop down on the ground and face him. The thought whispers across my mind that I should tell him none of this is his fault. I need to reassure him that I don't blame him for making us leave Cassian. He deserves that. But I can't look at him and say the words. No matter that my head tells me to utter them, my heart refuses. It's too soon, my grief is too fresh and I can't give voice to it. Instead, I walk past him.

I see Lia and Miram silhouetted in the distance, standing beside two electric lanterns. Several sleeping bags sit near them but they make no move to unfold them.

Will's footsteps sound behind me. I sigh, knowing I can't ignore him forever. I don't *want* to ignore him. I want everything to be right between us again, but I'm not sure that will be possible just now. I can't just stick my head in the sand and pretend that I'm okay. I might have chosen Will, but Cassian is—*was*—a part of me. And what does it mean for me and Will if I don't feel free to express my grief?

I open my mouth to speak, still not sure what to say. Words die in my throat as I spot Lia beginning to strip off her clothes. Immediately, I understand. I know that she's leaving us.

Miram, however, doesn't have a clue. 'What are you doing?' she demands, eyeing the girl like she's lost her mind.

Lia shrugs one bone-thin shoulder as if it were obvious. 'Going home.' Her blue-black eyes lock on mine. Kicking free of her too-big shorts, she folds her clothes into a tight bundle, tying the sleeves of her shirt together so nothing escapes, creating a sort of handle.

Facing me, she squares her shoulders. 'Thank you. You saved my life. I'll never forget that. Or you.'

'Are you sure?' I ask, worry for her knotting my chest. 'Do you know how to—'

'I know my way home.'

Again, I try. She's so young. It doesn't feel right to let her go off alone. 'But you can't fly during the day. What will you—'

'I'll lie low in daylight. It shouldn't take me long to get home. A couple of days. I'll be fine.' She smiles confidently, and I realize she isn't a child. Not any more. Who could be after living as a captive of the enkros?

And I know she'll be fine. She's a water draki. She'll never stray too far from a water source. It will offer her protection if she needs it. For a brief moment, I think to suggest she stay with us, but what can we offer her except risk and instability? She's probably better anywhere else.

'Good-bye, Lia,' I say. 'Take care.'

'Oh, I will. The rest of my life will be very dull, I promise you that.'

I smile a little. 'That does sound like heaven.'

She surprises me with a quick hug before turning and walking a few steps, her human exterior melting away as she manifests into the deep blue of a water draki. Then she's gone, springing up into the night. I watch the dark gleaming blue of her body until it's indistinguishable against the night sky.

Watching her go is another weight, a bit more added grief, knowing that I'll never see her again—never know for certain if she made it home and claimed that dull life for herself.

'C'mon, Miram,' Tamra says gently. 'Let's unroll these sleeping bags.' My sister glances at Will. 'Got any food?'

He nods and turns back to the van.

The mention of food makes my stomach growl, but my weariness wins out. I move my heavy limbs. Dropping down, I unroll my sleeping blankets and slide inside, feeling the need to do something to get away . . . even if it's pretend sleep. Facing Will right now, telling him what's in my heart—or rather what's not, what's dead and lost—that's simply too much.

Only I don't end up pretending. The moment my head hits the ground exhaustion takes hold and I'm gone.

I wake abruptly, every nerve in my body wired tight. A strange sense of exhilaration hums through me. I sit up, the plastic-slick fabric of my sleeping bag sliding to my waist with a scratchy whisper.

I scan the area around me. Miram and Tamra sleep nearby. For a moment I admire the flow of my sister's hair, a silvery waterfall spilling across the ground. I've gotten used to the sight of it. I no longer think of her as the *new* Tamra. She's simply Tamra. My sister. A relieved breath shudders past my lips. At least I haven't lost her.

And you still have Will.

At this reminder, my gaze crawls, searching for him.

I find him. Watching me. He sits with his back to a tree, one leg bent so that his arm drapes over his knee. I can almost believe he's been waiting for me to wake.

I sit up a little straighter. 'Will.'

The soft sound of my voice jars in the dead quiet of the wood. I glance at the sleeping girls, worried I woke them. They don't move.

'Why are you awake?' I ask.

'Just sitting over here thinking.'

I lick my lips. 'About what?'

He stares at me for a long minute across the distance, his hazel eyes nothing more than two dark gleams. 'About how you will always wonder if I wanted to leave him behind.'

My breath catches and it takes me a moment to respond. When I do, I'm glad at the steadiness of my voice. 'Did you?' I ask, even though I don't suspect for a moment that he did. That's not Will.

He shakes his head against the tree. 'I did what he wanted me to do, Jacinda. I saw it in his eyes. It was all I could do.'

I nod slowly. 'That's true.'

His eyes narrow and penetrate me. 'But that's not good enough for you.'

'I don't blame you.'

'You don't have to. I can see it in your eyes. You won't even let me so much as touch your hand . . .' His voice fades.

He thinks I blame him for losing Cassian? I rise from the sleeping bag, determined to correct him of that misapprehension. I may have been mad at him at first, in the moment, but I knew even then that he'd done the only thing he could for the rest of us to survive.

He watches with steady intensity as I approach him, my feet crackling over dried leaves. 'What are you doing?'

he asks as I lower myself down beside him, determined to prove to him that I'm not angry with him . . . that I believe in him. In us. I've been so caught up in hiding my grief from him . . . afraid to hurt him by revealing my pain. Turns out I've been hurting him anyway.

'Showing you,' I say.

'Showing me what?'

'That we're all right. I know you would have saved him if you could. I didn't mean for you to think I blamed you. I've been avoiding you because I felt guilty.'

'Guilty for what?'

'For missing Cassian. For feeling so . . . sad.' I shake my head. *Sad* seems such an inadequate word. I've forever lost a part of me. Part of me is dead. Cassian materializes in my head and it's like a physical blow. Like a punch directly to the stomach and I can't catch my breath. My chest rises raggedly, struggling for air. A fiery lock of hair falls before my eyes.

'You don't have to pretend you're not grieving. Don't feel guilty for feeling. For . . .' He pauses, and I see that his next words are a struggle for him. 'Don't feel guilty for caring about him, too.'

My heart squeezes and I know loving Will is right. It's always been right. For him to say those words only proves that my instincts have never been wrong about us—about him. He would never do anything to deliberately hurt anyone. Not me. Not even Cassian.

Will brushes the lock of hair back from my eyes, his look tender. 'Jacinda,' he whispers. 'You don't have to prove anything to me.' His brow furrows. 'Especially since I'm not as convinced as you are.'

I frown. 'What do you mean?'

He sighs and his expression tightens as though he were in physical pain. 'I keep replaying that final moment in my mind, asking myself if there was some way . . . if we didn't *have* to leave him behind.'

I cup his face in my hands and force him to look at me, determined that he hear me. 'You did everything you could.'

'How are you so confident of that?'

'Because you wouldn't be here beating yourself up about it if you did it on purpose. And you wouldn't hurt me.'

And that's the truth of it. That's been the truth since day one. Since we first met. He wouldn't harm Cassian if it would hurt me. I know that.

My thumb grazes his lower lip, tracing its shape, memorizing its smooth texture. His lids drift shut, and I bring my mouth closer. His mouth parts and I taste the warmth of his breath.

His eyes open, and they're darker than moments before and I feel a shot of satisfaction at my effect on him.

I scoot closer and drop my hand to his chest, kissing him tenderly, slowly at first. Pulling back, I look into his eyes again, so close to my own. They gleam darkly. I lean in for another kiss and he stops me with a firm hand on the shoulder.

'What?'

'You don't have to do this.'

I shake my head. 'Don't you want me—'

He squeezes his eyes tightly. He shoots a glance to where Miram and Tamra sleep and then blows out a frustrated breath. Suddenly he stands and seizes my hand, dragging me after him, weaving us through trees. Our legs cut through tall grass. He catches me when I stumble over a fallen branch. Both his arms surround me, solid and warm. I look up into his face and lose myself in the dark glitter of his eyes. His eyes are so clear, but the rest of his face is hazy, all shadowy lines and hollows.

The deep velvet of his voice strokes me and I lean toward him. 'I want you, Jacinda. With everything that I am. With my every breath. But you lost someone important to you today and you don't have to do anything to convince me of your love.' His breath rattles a little, the warm air brushing my cheek.

I sag against him then and release the tears I've been holding back in his presence. I clutch his shirt until my fingers are aching and bloodless. His arms tighten around me, holding me up.

Will is a good person. Plain and simple. Otherwise he wouldn't be here, holding me as I grieve for Cassian. He'd still be with his family of hunters. And I'd probably have died months ago.

And suddenly the need to kiss him is everything. Everything right and real. The balm to my many wounds.

My lips find his. Warm tears seep from my eyelids as our mouths fuse hotly. His hand slides through my hair. My own hands rove everywhere, touching, feeling, revelling in the strong, firm sensation of him. He makes a growling sound against my lips and my pulse skitters wildly at my throat.

Tears slide down my cheeks, the salty taste of them mingling in our kiss. Emotions war inside me, hunger, desire for him—and a broken heart for Cassian. I never would have thought such feelings could exist simultaneously. But, somehow, being with Will, losing myself in the heat of our kiss . . . it eases the ache inside my chest.

I press my mouth against his, focused on him, on the fusion of our lips, the sensation of his hand on the back of my head, his long fingers running through the snarls of my hair. I can't remember the last time I brushed it. I must look a mess, but he still wants me.

I lose myself to taste and sensation. To Will. I don't notice the shift in wind, the lift of my hair off my shoulders, the rustle of leaves in the trees . . . or the scent of something else on the air until it's too late.

Miram's scream cuts through the night, jolting me back to the present.

CHAPTER TEN

As I tear through the trees, my breath crashes from my lips and fear rides high in my chest at what I might find. *Let Tamra be OK. And Miram, too. I can't lose Cassian's sister; not after he died to save her.* Smoke gusts from my nose as Will and I explode back into the campsite at the same time.

I spot my sister immediately, standing protectively in front of Miram. Already fully manifested, Tamra is swathed in a fine cloud of vapour. As a shader, it's all she has. A great defence when dealing with humans, but it offers no protection or defence when confronting one of our own kind. She can't shade another draki.

And it's a draki she faces.

I shake my head, unable to reconcile what I see. The grey draki stands, all heaving muscle and rippling sinew, before my sister. The only thing reassuring about the sight of him is that his skin lies flat and smooth, not lifted into countless blades over his body. But I know it only takes him an instant to arm for attack. I remember this well, and fear for Tamra shudders through me, too strong to resist.

I manifest, my wings surging, tearing through my shirt, my sister's name a cry on my lips.

The grey draki looks over his shoulder at me, but makes no move, even as his gaze narrows with recognition.

Will stands beside me, his arm brushing mine.

'Why are you here?' I demand. 'You're free.' He can go anywhere. Why is he stalking us?

He looks back at Tamra. He stares at her as if he's never seen anything like her before. My stomach quivers with unease. He looks at her like she's a tasty snack he'd like to sample.

'You're free,' Tamra echoes. 'You can go.'

He finally looks away, but not at any of us. He looks up at the sky, stretching his throat.

I follow his gaze. At first I see nothing but dark night, then a sound reaches my ears—like great smacks of wind hitting a sail. I'd recognize it anywhere. A draki in flight.

Then it's like the night itself moves—black liquid spilling over air that's nearly as dark. Nearly but not quite. I make out the wings, the glow of eyes I know so well.

'Cassian,' I breathe.

He touches down without a sound, moving slower than usual—clearly injured. He nods once at the grey draki in a silent acknowledgment of sorts.

They're together? How is that possible? Last time we saw them they were trying to kill each other.

'Cassian,' Miram cries and vaults across the distance, flinging herself into her brother's arms. My muscles tense, wanting to do the same. But I hesitate. Things are

87

complicated enough. While I'm thrilled and relieved that he's alive, I'm aware of Will beside me.

I edge closer to Cassian. 'You're not dead?'

'Apparently not.'

Then I can't help myself. I'm hugging him, feeling all the solid sensation of him for myself. 'But you were in pain . . . I felt that . . . and then there was suddenly nothing. Emptiness. You . . . died.'

'The enkros came. I was still awake. Just dazed from the gas. They took me out with some kind of a tranquillizer.'

I step back, dropping my arms, putting distance between us as I look from him to the grey draki. 'And what? You're friends now? How'd you both get here?'

Cassian rotates his neck and glances around, the motion weary.

'When I came to, he was fighting them off. The gas didn't work on him. He saved us both. We escaped through the tunnel you all left behind. They didn't know what to make of it and had immediately begun to tear through it.'

He shrugs one large, muscled shoulder. 'I think they thought you all might have been hiding on the other side.' His gaze swings to Will and he bobs his head in a nod of thanks. And I know he's thanking Will for more than the tunnel. He's thanking him for saving me, for saving his sister. All of us.

He's thanking Will for listening and leaving him behind. Will can't understand a word he's saying, but I see in his face that he understands this.

I jerk a thumb toward the grey draki again. 'And now you trust him?'

'I wouldn't have made it out of there without him. He broke free first and took out several of the enkros guarding us.' He looks down at himself. 'Do you have any clothes handy?'

I motion to the van, assuming his things are still in there. He takes off towards it in long strides, his sister following.

I turn my attention back to the grey draki. He looks in no hurry to demanifest, still staring at Tamra with such sole focus that annoyance begins to heat and prick at my skin. I'm not sure I could demanifest right now even if I willed it.

Tamra doesn't look wholly comfortable with the attention she's getting either. She glances around herself and bends down, gathering her clothes, mostly ruined. She holds them self-consciously to her chest and edges away, walking backwards from this draki that can't stop staring at her as though he might gobble her up at any moment.

She darts towards the van where Cassian and Miram disappeared, leaving me, Will, and the grey one alone.

He steps forward as though he might follow Tamra. I block his path, my chest heaving, the smoulder eating its way up my windpipe. I shake my head in warning at him.

His eyes flare as he comes face-to-face with me. He remembers me well.

'She's my sister,' I announce as if that should squash his interest in her. He did try to kill me, after all— something I haven't forgotten, no matter that I might sympathize with his motivation at the time. He looks from me to her retreating figure and back at me again.

And still, he holds himself maddeningly silent.

'Don't you have somewhere else to go?' I wave a hand, motioning in the direction Lia took. 'You're free.'

A low rumble rises from his chest, not quite a growl, but close.

I angle my head. 'What? You don't speak?'

'Jacinda, what are you doing? Trying to irritate him?' Will moves up beside me, ready to jump into any potential fray that may erupt. He can't understand my words but he recognizes my provoking tone. His square jaw clenches tightly, a muscle feathering the flesh of his cheek.

The rumble comes again, even less growllike, almost like the draki tongue . . . and then I realize it *is* the draki tongue. The sound is a little rusty from disuse and neglect, but it's undeniably draki speech. 'Listen to the human. Don't get in my face, fire-breather.'

His voice, so deep and guttural, startles me—more than the threat of his words. Footsteps sound behind me and I see that Tamra approaches hesitantly, dressed in a T-shirt and jeans, looking both normal and eerily beautiful with her frosty eyes and silvery hair.

Her wide eyes raptly fix on the grey draki in front of me. She looks less uncomfortable now. I frown. Less uncomfortable and more intrigued, and this only makes *me* uncomfortable. I don't know anything about this guy except that he's built for killing—the perfect weapon. But then, so am I.

'Maybe we should demanifest,' I suggest, glancing from his body to mine, glimmering in the night. 'That might make us both feel easier.'

He angles his head and gives me a funny look. 'I'm not uneasy.'

Of course not. He can sprout a thousand blades all over his body in a mere heartbeat. Why should *he* feel uneasy?

'Just demanifest,' I snap.

It's a long while before he answers. 'I don't know how.'

I'm slow to process his words, but once I do, I pull back, needing the distance, not feeling safe so close to this draki that is essentially a dragon.

'What?' Will asks, immediately registering my reaction and knowing something is wrong. 'Can you demanifest and talk to me? Tell me what's going on?'

'She asked him to demanifest and he said he can't,' Tamra explains, stepping closer to me. But she's careful to stay behind me. Like she's afraid of getting too close to this draki.

'What do you mean?' I demand.

He doesn't know how? How is that possible? That's what we are—what a draki does. The human part of us is every bit as real as the draki.

'It's been too long,' he says. 'I don't remember how.'

I look him up and down. 'How long have you been like this?'

'Since they captured me and my pride.'

They captured his *entire* pride?

As though he can read my mind, he continues, 'My pride had been hunted for so long. We were just a handful at the end. Seventeen of us. No children. Now I'm all that's left.'

I shudder, thinking of this, of how it must feel to be captured alongside of everyone you know and love, family and friends. To lose them all. 'How long were you a prisoner?' I repeat, an ache starting in my chest.

He shakes his head, tossing his ash blond waves. His hair falls past his shoulders—as matted and wild as the rest of him. 'I can't know for sure,' he says in that raspy voice. 'You don't count the days in there. It's not possible. It feels as though I spent several lifetimes in those walls.'

I nod, well remembering how the single day I spent in that cell felt so much longer. Forever.

'I watched my kin die all around me. They either faded away until death claimed them or the enkros killed them with their experiments. I wished for death, so that I could be free, too.' He tilts his face up to the night, clearly savouring the wind on his face. The ridges along his nose flex with breath.

'And now you are free,' I say.

'It's been so long. I was fourteen when I went in.' His lips twist, the top lip curling over a flash of bone-white teeth.

Tamra gasps behind me.

He levels that smile of sorts on her. 'I'm guessing I don't look fourteen any longer?'

No. No, he doesn't. He looks hardened and experienced. Probably older than I am.

He's been with them for years. My thoughts reel. At least four years, I would guess. And a draki all this time. No wonder he's so primitive . . . such a savage.

Will and Tamra talk in low voices as she translates everything that's been said.

Cassian returns then, and I'm relieved. I don't know what else to say to this nameless draki, a wild animal freed from his cage. The way he's acted . . . it's no surprise.

'He needs a place to go,' Cassian announces in a voice that rings with the confidence of one destined to rule, and dominate, especially if Severin has any say. 'We'll take him with us.'

I swing around. 'To the pride?'

I'm not sure about this. Even if I feel slightly more empathetic towards him, it's a lot to forget the danger he poses.

'Where else?' Cassian asks. 'He can't demanifest.' Apparently the draki explained his situation to Cassian, too. 'We can't just leave him here on his own.'

And then I remember that I'm not going back. When I left the pride I had no intention of ever returning, and now that Cassian can escort Miram home, there's no need to. I shouldn't care if Cassian wants to take a wild beast back to the pride.

But I do.

It's not a switch I can flip off. I care about Cassian and Az and countless others still living in the pride. Taking this draki there could risk them all.

I look Cassian over. His breathing is laboured. He's still hurting, one hand clutching his side. How's he going to handle Miram and a draki that can't demanifest? All on his own? 'He's a little unpredictable, isn't he?'

'Leaving him like this would be irresponsible,' Cassian says with a wave towards him. 'He has no pride. No-where to go. He can't be cut loose. He'll either be captured again or end up harming someone.'

'Jacinda, it's the right thing to do,' Tamra inserts.

I growl now. From frustration at this entire situation. From my sister's altruism.

Then I feel bad because I know it's not fair to think that way. She's here because of me. When we left home, she would have been happy to leave the pride behind forever and search for Mum. I persuaded her to delay that plan on Miram's behalf. I owe it to her to listen to her opinion.

With that thought, I bite back the urge to disagree and stalk away to the van to locate more clothes—and try to cool down enough to demanifest.

Will stays behind with the others, his wary gaze still on the grey draki, and I know he won't drop his guard even for a moment. Not just because he senses my unease, but because he's smart that way. As a hunter, willing or not, he possesses his own share of well-honed instincts.

This mollifies me a little.

Until my gaze lands on Cassian. My chin lifts as I convey to him that he should really reconsider taking this draki home with him. His jaw locks tightly with resolution. Still, I try to reach him. I communicate with my eyes . . . with the bond that hums between us. And I sigh. No matter what, there is always that. No matter what I have with Will. I have something with Cassian, too.

CHAPTER ELEVEN

Stepping out of sight from the others, I round the van. Embracing my solitude, I take a deep breath, dragging cool air into my burning lungs for several moments. The heat subsides, and so do I. My wings ease back down, disappearing between my shoulder blades with a crack of bone and cartilage . . . until the next time.

'Here you go.'

I jump a little at the sound of Will's voice. Turning, I accept the shirt he stretches out for me and pull it over my head. 'Thanks.'

'Are you OK?' His eyes drill into mine.

'Yes. Sure. Cassian's alive.' I'm shaky inside as I say this and I realize that it's just hitting me. Cassian. Alive. *Not dead.* My legs wobble, ready to give out.

The arrival of the grey draki eclipses my relief. Looking at him is like seeing what I could be, what we all could be—draki everywhere—if we were kept captive for years and treated like wild animals. And the way he is staring at Tamra just gives me a bad feeling.

Will stares at me soberly. 'We're parting ways with them, Jacinda. Remember? You shouldn't feel responsible for them.'

'Yeah.' I nod, even if I'm not convinced. Cassian's emotions run strong, pulling at me. He believes he needs me to get back to the pride. Needs . . . or wants. I'm not sure which. Maybe both.

I inhale. And that's when I smell him. That aroma that is distinctly Will. Standing so close to him again, I feel my chest grow tight and achy. There were moments in the last twenty-four hours where I doubted I'd ever have this again. I tilt my face up to him. Everywhere Will's gaze roams feels like a touch, a caress.

Soon it will be just me and Will. And Tam. We'll be safe. And we'll find Mum. Everything will be all right.

Still, the unease lingers in me.

My scalp tingles and tightens knowing the grey draki is just a few yards away. And Cassian intends to take him back to the pride, when he's hardly fit to get himself back there.

And even more than that. Something still seems wrong. I worry we haven't entirely escaped. We may not be free yet. It still feels like something is . . . coming.

As if sensing my bleak thoughts, Will steps closer. His hands slide up and down my arms. I look up into his face and lose myself in the deep sea of his eyes.

'Everything has worked out. We're on our way, just like we planned. And not a moment too soon.' One corner of his mouth curls. 'I've waited long enough to get you alone.'

And I can't say the words burning inside me with his hopeful gaze locked on me. I can't tell him that deep in my core, in the marrow of my bones, I don't feel like any of this is over yet.

I hide my feelings with a smile. 'We won't be too alone. There will still be my sister.'

He grins. 'She likes me—'

'You think?' I tease.

'I know. Don't go trying to put doubts in my head.' His fingers dance along my ribs, tickling my side. Even this light touch leaves me breathless—and not because I'm ticklish. I jerk and bounce sideways but he follows me, pulling me flush against him and backing us both against the van. 'She likes me and will take pity on me to give us a moment alone now and then.' His gaze scans my face, warming my skin.

'Oh, really?'

'Yes.'

'Good,' I tease back. 'You still owe me that date. Dinner. A movie.'

The laughter in those hazel eyes fades, and his gaze grows intent and serious. Desire brims there. The longing of someone who has waited too long already. 'What about you? Will you take pity and ease my suffering?' He buries his nose in my hair and inhales deeply.

'How have you been suffering?' I whisper, my vanity craving the words.

'I suffer for you . . . from wanting you and only getting these stolen moments here and there.'

As if to prove his point, the sound of my name stretches on the wind. 'Jacinda!'

Will groans and drops his head into his palm. 'See what I mean?'

Tamra approaches, her hair glistening like pearls in the moonlight. 'Ah, there you are. Cassian thinks we should get moving again . . . that we're still too close to the enkros stronghold.'

I bite back my question: *Since when do you care what Cassian wants?* I stop myself though. Better that he affects her so little that she can speak his name as if he'd never broken her heart.

'Sure,' I say, squeezing past the warm solidity of Will's chest with a sigh. I'd like nothing more than to curl up and sleep with him as my pillow.

Tamra moves away. I hear the door at the back of the van creak open and I start to head that way, not wanting to leave my sister alone with a draki who looks at her like she's his first glimpse of sunlight. Will stops me and quickly tugs me back into his arms for a heated kiss. His lips. On mine. It's everything. I revel in the feel of his hands, the texture of his roughened palms as they hold my face. His thumbs pressing lightly into my cheeks. I melt against him.

When we finally break for air, he whispers against my hair, 'It's just until we reach the truck stop where we left the car. Hang on until then.'

His words wash me in cold. I should speak up now and let him know that I'm worried about leaving Cassian injured with the burden of Miram and the grey draki.

But I can't find my voice yet. And maybe Cassian will have recovered enough before we reach the truck stop. We heal quickly, after all. I flex my fingers against the cool cotton of his T-shirt and hold him close for a moment longer. 'Don't worry about me. I'll be fine.'

We're cramped inside the back of the van. Even with Miram sitting up front with Will, Cassian and the grey draki take up a lot of room. Especially a fully manifested draki.

Cassian insisted that Miram sit up front, claiming she'd been confined in a cell long enough. As it was a rather wretched experience—my brief stay in the enkros stronghold can attest to that—I didn't argue.

The grey draki seems too huge. He devours all the space, sucks everything inside himself, leaving Tamra and me pressed close together. I think longingly of that front passenger seat that Miram now occupies.

'So do you have a name?' Tamra surprises me by asking *him*. Her tone was a little too friendly for my taste. I shoot her a look. She meets my gaze and shrugs. Keeping my watchful gaze on him, I resist rolling my eyes. He must have a name. He did exist somewhere else, presumably in this country, before the enkros took him.

He nods once. 'Deghan,' he says.

Deghan. An old-sounding name. And it fits him perfectly.

'Why don't you concentrate on trying to demanifest while you're stuck back here?' Cassian suggests.

Deghan looks at Cassian and his lips curl almost with disgust. I can't blame him. Who wants to openly struggle, in front of an audience, to do something he can't?

'Maybe another time,' Tamra quickly inserts, her voice softly comforting. 'You've just forgotten how is all. It will come back to you.'

Deghan watches her intently, his pewter dragon eyes devouring. I can't fathom his thoughts. I only know that I don't like that he watches her. Period.

We stop at a diner in the middle of nowhere. The sound of traffic on the two-lane highway is sporadic. I smell the aroma of cooking meat on the wind before Will even opens one of the doors. My stomach grumbles. We shared a bag of powdered doughnuts this morning—hardly the stuff of champions. We could all use some real food. Bright light slants in through the back doors and I squint at the intrusion.

'Obviously, we can't all go in and sit down to eat,' Will announces, glancing over his shoulder to make sure no one wanders close and happens to spot a seven-foot winged creature in the back of the van. 'Jacinda and I can order food for everyone and bring it back.' He nods his head, indicating that I should climb out.

I step down and we walk across the parking lot. Loose gravel crunches under my shoes. It's a long walk. Will parked at the back of the lot, far from the doors and prying eyes.

'Thanks,' I murmur. 'Nice to get a break from back there.'

'Figured as much,' he replies, slipping his hand around mine. 'And Miram doesn't seem eager to surround herself with humans. She's not exactly chatty with me up there.'

We order burgers and fries in the diner. I make sure to order extra, knowing how Cassian eats and guessing Deghan has an equally ravenous appetite.

Sitting on stools at the counter, waiting for our order, I almost feel normal. Since Tamra interrupted us the last time we were alone, it's nice to have this time together.

'Would you like drinks while you wait?' a waitress behind the counter asks. At our nods, she pours and leaves us with two sodas sweating in plastic red glasses.

I fiddle with a straw. 'This might be the closest we get to a real sit-down date for a while.'

He shakes his head. 'Not exactly what I had in mind. We can do better.' He winks at me. 'We will.'

Tearing the paper off the extra straw, I smooth it semi-flat with my fingers until it's just right. Bringing one end to my lips, I carefully cup my hands, positioning them into the perfect pocket, and begin to blow out a tune. Lowering my hands, I ask, 'Impressed?'

'You have no idea.'

I nod in satisfaction. 'Just wait. It gets better.' Next, I start whistling the tune of 'Camptown Races.'

'Okay,' he says with mock seriousness. 'Now you're just turning me on.'

I almost mess up, tempted to giggle at that. Finished, I lean back with a flourish and grin. He claps.

'Didn't know about that particular talent of mine, did you?' I preen, enjoying myself.

'It puts your other . . . *abilities* to shame.'

I laugh, and swivel on the stool. It feels so *normal*, so right and good to be with him like this. Happy and silly and carefree. I can almost pretend the others aren't out there waiting on us. He catches my legs and stops me. His face is solemn as he leans in to kiss me with those cool, smooth lips of his, not even caring if anyone watches us. I grasp the edge of his jacket with my fingers, pulling him closer, deepening the kiss, wishing we were alone.

After a moment, we break apart. My breath catches. He's always been good-looking, but I'd forgotten the effect of that smile. The blinding flash of white teeth. The deep grooves along his mouth. It's one of the first genuine smiles I've seen from him since we escaped the stronghold and my heart squeezes. The variable colour of his eyes shines like gemstones. As though he can read my mind, he utters, 'It will be us soon. Like this. With all the time in the world. And you can teach me how to make straw music.'

We walk back, arms heavy with hot bags of food, grease leaking through the white paper. At Miram's window, we pass her food for both her and Will. She smiles a grudging thanks. It's something. Now that Cassian is back, maybe she appreciates everything I did to help rescue her. Maybe things will be different between us now. An unexpected lump rises in my throat as I realize that I would like that.

Before Will opens the back door he presses a kiss to my temple. 'Tomorrow we'll be free.'

I inhale again. Tomorrow. Eagerness trips through me as I think of all the moments I'll have with Will just like the one we shared in the diner. But even better because the kissing and talking doesn't have to stop.

He closes his fingers around the door handle to pull it open, then pauses.

I freeze, too, studying him as a predatory stillness comes over him.

'What?'

He holds up a hand as if he needs total silence to listen.

I angle my head and scan the parking lot. There's nothing in the great stretch of dark gravel except a random assortment of cars and trucks. An occasional customer enters and exits the diner. Yet Will's features look tight, his hazel eyes intense as he scours the area.

'Will? What is it?'

He shakes his head, sending his brown hair tossing against his forehead. 'Nothing, I guess.'

He opens the van door and helps me inside. My last glimpse of him before he closes the door only cements in my mind that something still bothers him, but I don't know what.

Turning around, I hand everyone food and settle down to eat. I nibble on the end of a fry and try to ignore the tight itchy sensation rippling over my scalp.

CHAPTER TWELVE

It's imperceptible at first. Just a slight increase in the van's speed. The faintest swelling growl of the engine. Then we take a turn and all of us slide to one side of the van, food flying everywhere. My head bumps the hard floor.

Tamra topples against Deghan and the solid, muscled bands of his arms wrap around her. I cringe at the sight, but there's not much I can do from my position, sprawled against the cold metal floor.

Other sounds grow on the air over the roar of the van: the whoosh of wind and honking horns from other traffic as Will weaves in and out.

'What's going on?' Tamra hollers. 'Why's he driving like a maniac?'

There's only one reason. Fire erupts in my core, climbing up my throat. Char lines my mouth.

Cassian announces what I already know in my gut. 'Someone's after us.'

The little colour present in Tamra's face bleeds out at

this revelation. Glints of pearl flash beneath her skin. 'Enkros?'

Cassian's pupils shudder to thin vertical slits. He shakes his head. 'I don't—'

'Enkros don't do their own hunting,' I say between numb lips.

My gaze clashes with Cassian. I feel his tension, his readiness, but no fear. Not like what I felt when he was a prisoner of the enkros.

His lips move, uttering the word that races around my mind. 'Hunters.'

Tamra releases a shuddery breath. Deghan touches her arm, a surprising show of . . . I'm not sure what. Support? Comfort? I don't know. It's still hard to reconcile him with the draki that tried to kill me. My natural inclination is not to like him. The back of my throat prickles with the urge to blast him with steam. And yet, he's gentle with Tamra.

Will swerves and we're tossed again. My shoulder hits the wall and I cry out. Then we still, jerking to an abrupt halt. I lift myself up, my arms quivering. The stink of burning tyres fills my nose.

'Jacinda!' Cassian's there, sliding an arm around me and helping me into a sitting position. 'Are you all right?'

I nod, still shaking and a little dizzy. 'S-should we get out?' I ask, wondering what's happening outside the van.

I feel the slam of Will's door more than I hear it. It rocks the entire van.

The doors suddenly open to a flood of light. Will looks anxiously in at us. Miram, her face pale with the panic that we all feel, quickly appears beside him.

'I've lost them,' Will announces. 'But they're not far behind.'

'Hunters?'

Will nods. 'Yeah.' Dust floats on the air from the van's wild ride. He looks over his shoulder, peering first down the small rural road we sit parked on and then scanning the tall trees sandwiching us on the narrow road.

'They'll catch up soon. Go. Run.' With a shake of his head, he waves to the trees. 'If they find you, just act like you're hiking. They won't suspect anything if they just bump into a bunch of kids. It's your only chance. We can meet up at the truck stop where I left my car. It's not too far. Remember the place?'

Cassian nods.

Will looks almost apologetically at Deghan. 'You're out of luck, buddy. Too bad you can't change. You better fly away, hide, whatever you can do. Stay out of sight.'

Deghan jerks his head once in understanding. He's clearly accustomed to fending on his own. And I almost feel a sense of relief. If we lose him that would take care of my worry for the pride.

Will squats and presses his fingers to the ground, his expression one of intense concentration as he feels for those approaching.

My heart thumps madly against my chest, instantly understanding what he's doing and marvelling that he should have this ability to connect to the earth to such a degree. As any earth draki might. Perhaps more. It's almost as if he alone can hear the earth's whisper.

'What about you?' I demand, dread clawing its way through me at the idea of separating from Will again. *Not again.*

He straightens, his eyes softening as they look at me, reminding me of moss growing on water-soaked river rocks. 'They won't hurt me—'

I surge toward him and seize both his hands in mine. 'No! I'm not leaving you.'

'They're not after me, Jacinda.' The determination in his gaze cuts me. He won't be swayed.

'How did they track us?' Cassian mutters, looking at Will as if he might know.

Will's gaze shifts from me to Cassian. 'I don't know. The enkrós must have alerted them of the escape.' He waves a hand. 'They probably have hunters covering a wide radius out from the stronghold right now. It wouldn't be just my family but others, too.'

'What is this?' Deghan looks Will over suspiciously. 'His family hunts us?'

'His family. Not him,' I explain.

Deghan fails to look entirely appeased.

'I know how you feel. It took me a while to accept that there is a distinction between him and them,' Cassian volunteers.

I take a relieved breath. It's the first time I've heard Cassian admit Will is different.

Will fixes his stare on me, his hazel eyes unwavering and full of a purpose that almost convinces me that everything will be OK once I dive into those trees. 'If they come across you, act like you have nothing to hide. If I can, I'll meet you all at the truck stop.'

If I can . . .

The words echo in my head as I contemplate the various scenarios that would keep him from me. None good.

'Yeah, sure you will,' Miram growls, the sound of her voice unexpected. She's said so little since we left the stronghold. 'You and your family.'

'Miram,' Cassian says gently.

'Hasn't he done enough to prove his loyalty?' I demand, my hands curling into fists. 'What's it going to take?'

'Oh, when are you going to see he'll always be one of them?' Miram explodes, her eyes flashing with more animation than I've ever seen from her. 'If your little stay with the enkros didn't teach you the difference between us and them—'

'Then nothing will,' I finish, my voice hard. 'Precisely. Nothing ever will.'

She stares at me as if she can't comprehend me. And I imagine she can't.

'Jacinda . . .' She works her hands, waving them in the air. 'You'll never be compatible.'

'Enough. Both of you,' Cassian bites out. 'We've got hunters bearing down on us, intent on skinning us alive . . . or turning us over to those bastards that wanted to open me up back there.' He motions behind us.

I look desperately at Will, my chest heaving with hot emotion.

I start to shake my head, determined to stay with him, when Cassian says my name sharply, the command swift. 'Jacinda.' His gaze cuts straight into me. 'You're coming with us.'

I bristle at his tone. And then I feel his fury. It pours through me, thick as tar. Buried amid the rage, I feel something else as he glares down at me. Another emotion. Just as hot. Just as intense. *Fear.* For me. My temper cools. He's been through a lot on account of me.

'Jacinda?' Will's voice snatches my attention. 'You need to get going.'

I fight my panic that I'm leaving Will. *Again.* Eyes burning, I nod, looking around for my sister even as my mind whirs, trying to come up with some way to remain with Will without upsetting everyone. I can't get separated from him again.

With her jaw set at a stubborn angle, Tamra watches me, waiting for my next move. The sight punches me like a fist. She won't go without me. Regret washes over me, prickling my flesh with needles of heat. I can't endanger my sister. I've already lost Mum. I can't risk losing her, too. I have to get her off this road, and then I'll come back for Will.

I look back to Will. 'I'll find you,' I announce, my tone implying he better be somewhere I can find him. Either here or at his car.

'I'll be waiting.' He nods, looking anxiously back down the road.

And that's when we hear them. The rumble of engines coming. *How is it they're tracking us?*

'Go!' His gaze sweeps over us before resting on me, urging me to move. 'Go! Now!'

The others turn and flee, crashing through the trees like a herd of elephants in their haste. I wince.

Will snags my attention again, sliding his fingers through my hair and tugging me against him for a quick, hard kiss. I revel in the feel of his mouth on mine, the curve of his hands against my scalp. He comes up for air and whispers hotly against my lips, 'Be safe. Take care of yourself out there.'

I open my mouth to give him the same advice, but the distant hum of engines makes me jerk and squint down the dirt road. I don't see anything yet. Just a cloud of brown.

Without looking at me, Will stands back and pushes me toward the trees. 'Go. They're coming!'

I run for the trees, my heart ready to burst from my chest.

My skin sparks with heat. Bursts of red-gold colour my human skin in hot flashes.

I dive into the cover of trees. The foliage immediately swallows me. I stop just inside the dark, clawing press of thick bushes and grass so wild it reaches my waist. There, I pause, listening to rustling all around me. I don't see any of the others, and this is OK as long as they're safe. As long as Tamra is safe. She has to be.

Just as I start to think that I'm on my own, that I've been left behind, I hear Cassian's whisper.

'Jacinda—what are you doing? Let's go!'

I spot him amid the trees, his face tight and anxious, flashing between his swarthy human skin and his charcoal black draki flesh. Behind him stands Miram, her small face an unremarkable beige smudge of fear.

I shake my head at him and look back towards the road.

I can't move. I have to see. Have to know. No matter what he told me to do. When it comes down to it, I'm not leaving Will. I swallow against the hot thickness of my throat. Not again.

CHAPTER THIRTEEN

Looking around, a plan begins to form. I spot a wide, heavily leafed tree with a slanting trunk for easy climbing. Tackling it, I make my way up with little effort, my fingers digging with ease into the bark.

'Jacinda.' Cassian's whisper is less discreet this time. He's moved and now stands below my tree. Miram follows, scowling up at me and worrying the edge of her shirt with her hands.

Cassian stabs a finger toward the ground like I should immediately come down to that spot.

'No. I'll be fine.' I give him a meaningful glare. 'Unless you give us away.' I wave at him. 'Now get out of here.'

He blows out a frustrated breath and turns back to his sister. 'Go. Hide. I'll find you.'

Terror flashes across her face. 'I don't want to go without you.'

'You'll be OK,' he says. 'Go deep in the woods and find Tamra. Just stay human.'

I snort. Last time she couldn't manage to do that.

He ignores me and continues with his instructions. 'You're safer out there. If they stumble upon you, they won't suspect . . .'

She shakes her head side to side; clearly the notion of them finding her freaks her out.

'Cassian,' I hiss down at him, 'you should go with her.'

He swipes a hand through the air to silence me. Looking at his sister, he commands, 'Go.'

With one last pleading look at him, she flees into the trees, her shoulders slumped like a woman headed to her execution.

He quickly climbs up a tree that practically crosses trunks with the one I'm hiding in.

'You're being stupid,' I whisper. Sending Miram away like that makes me feel uneasy. Like he's choosing me over his sister. I don't want him to do that. Ever. 'You should be with your sister.'

'And you're being so smart?' he counters, his purple dark gaze clashing with my own.

And then I feel it. Again. Confusing and bewildering, his desire sweeps over me in a warm wash, the sensation drugging. I shake my head, fighting to reclaim myself. My emotions, not his. Mine are enough to deal with—I don't need the interference of his. I arch against the invasion. Fighting it—him.

He looks at me starkly through the tangle of branches, our faces inches away even in our separate trees.

Engines growl closer, unmistakable. I peer through the branches. The ball of dust is larger; the vehicles, dark shapes at its centre.

By now, Will is occupying himself by looking beneath the hood. Is that his plan? Faking engine trouble? I inhale, hoping it will work.

In the thick nimbus of dirt, I pick out two vehicles. A black truck with windows so darkly tinted it's impossible to see inside. A van follows behind it, windows equally dark. This van is nothing like ours. Fully pimped out, it shines even submerged in the cloud of dirt.

Will peers out from beneath the hood, and I feel a stab of worry. Would the hunters hurt him? One of their own?

The vehicles stop and the engines die.

For a moment no one steps out and I wonder what they're doing in there. Their windows remind me of cold, dark eyes, silently watching and condemning. My chest rises and falls in fast pants. Steam releases from my nostrils in twin ribbons.

Will waves one hand in warm greeting, his wariness effectively masked. I hold still, suck in a breath, and trap it inside my too-tight chest, waiting for one of his family members to emerge.

Finally, the truck doors open, followed by the van doors. Several men step out. Five all together. I scan all of them . . . and recognize no one.

My pulse races at my neck, jumping against my flesh. My gaze flies to Will and I see he, too, finds them unfamiliar. Until this moment, I didn't realize how much I'd hoped they would be Will's family.

I shake my head and swat a strand of hair from my face. But if Will doesn't recognize them, then these hunters are not from Will's group. They're strangers. A stark sense of relief sweeps over me. They don't know Will.

He'll have a better chance persuading them he's just a stranded driver.

'Hey,' Will says, managing to look relieved and sheepish at the same time. Just a hapless teenager. 'Glad you guys showed up. Having a bit of car trouble here.' He pats the van's rusted side.

'Yeah?' One of the hunters steps to the front, his voice loud and jarring with unspoken challenge. Sunlight glints off the fine blond fuzz of his buzz cut. 'That a fact?' He glances around, eyeing our surroundings. His gaze skims over the spot where Cassian and I hide. I stiffen, clinging harder to the rough, scraping bark, blinking with relief that his attention doesn't linger in our direction.

Looking straight ahead again, he squints pale eyes at the back doors of our van as if he can somehow see within.

'Yeah.' Will gives a disarming laugh. 'Guess she's on her last breath.'

The lead hunter shares a look with his troop. A look that translates: *This guy is full of crap.* I fight to swallow against the thick surge of heat in my throat. They're not buying his story.

'Why don't you come clean with us, kid?' a hunter with a slicked-back ponytail and deeply pitted acne scars asks. 'You're not having car trouble.' He nods to the back of the van. 'What you got in there?'

And then I notice another hunter holding a strange device. Like a metal box except it's got some kind of antennae. From my vantage I can see a row of red blinking lights on the face of it. He turns with the box, rotating in a circle. Sometimes the red lights fade, depending on the way he faces—other times they begin flashing in earnest.

My gut twists sickly, and I know that box means trouble for us. I catch Cassian's gaze and see that he's noted it, too. His face is grim, features pulled tight.

I look back to Will, avoiding glancing at the box again. The sight of it panics me, and I need to stay calm. Calm. Cool. Draki buried.

I have to hand it to Will. He does a good job faking his bewilderment.

'What are you talking about?' He motions to the doors. 'I don't have anything back there. At the moment, it's empty. Usually it's full of equipment for my dad's landscaping business.' Now he looks embarrassed. 'But I, ah, had other plans for it this weekend so I emptied it.'

And then I know what I have to do. I start scrambling down from the tree.

Cassian whispers my name, his eyes wide as I drop down onto the soft ground. His anger reaches me. It's coupled with fear. The bitter taste of both coats my mouth, mingling with the rising ash and char inside me.

I look up at Cassian—my bonded mate whether I like it or not. His nose flattens out, ridges popping up along the bridge. Any second now he's going to be lost to his draki.

I shake my head at him and shoot him a look begging him to trust me. I *will* fix this. I put everything I feel into this plea, all my determination, all my confidence. Our eyes lock in silent communication. *I know what I'm doing.*

His shoulders sag and I know he's relented—hopefully he won't come charging after me. Glancing around, I see some squat, barely budded yellow wildflowers. They need a few more weeks to reach their full potential, but they'll have to do. I yank them free of the soil's grip and grab some weeds, hastily arranging them together in a semblance of a bouquet.

With one final glance at Cassian, I move towards the road, feeling the heat of his gaze as it burns into my back. Hopefully, he'll just sit tight and watch as I try to save us all.

CHAPTER FOURTEEN

They don't know you. They don't know you.

This is the mantra that runs over and over in my mind as I step out onto the road. Into the light and into the hunters' range of vision.

Will looks up first, proving that despite how blasé he comes across, he's very alert to the situation and our surroundings. Panic flashes across his eyes when he sees me, just for a second before vanishing.

'Hey,' one of the hunters exclaims when he spots me.

'Oh, good,' I say. 'You got help. I was worried we'd have to call my mum and that would have been so *not* cool.'

All the others turn to stare at me. Their shocked expressions are almost laughable. Females have no place in the world of hunters. In their eyes, by their rules, I shouldn't be here. My presence throws them off, which is precisely what I wanted.

'It's a girl,' one calls out.

'Uh, yeah,' I reply, the tone of my voice seeming to say *duh*. 'What were you expecting? A raccoon?' I giggle at my joke and stroll over to Will. 'Look at the flowers I found, baby.' I brandish my sloppy little bundle of wildflowers in the air like they're some sort of prize. They're really rather pathetic, already beginning to wilt, but I try to pretend the drooping stems are something more. Something worth oohing over.

Will slides a hand to the small of my back. 'Nice, babe.' He leans down and kisses me, long and deep. I feel the hunters' gazes on me and try not to let it creep me out. Our performance right now is important. It's everything.

'What are you doing here?' the leader asks, still looking confused.

'We were just out for a drive.' I frown and look at Will. 'Shouldn't you all be working on the van or something?'

Will looks back at the hunters. 'Any of you mind taking a look under the hood with me?'

'Forget that,' the ponytailed hunter snaps. 'We don't have time.' He turns to his leader. 'C'mon, let's go. We must have lost them—'

'No,' the guy holding the metal box protests. 'We're close.' He holds up the box to reveal the monitor with its flashing red lights. 'We've got at least one of them in close range!'

I stand on my tiptoes and peer at the box, trying not to look too interested.

'What you got there? Is that one of those treasure finders? You guys hunting down coins or something?' Will asks, managing to come off as no more than a nosy kid.

Buzz Cut shoots him a disgusted look and shakes his head. Otherwise, they ignore Will.

'Look, it's strong this way.' The guy holding the box moves to the edge of the road, in the direction we took into the woods. My hand tightens around Will's. He squeezes back. I can't help it. My gaze drifts upwards, towards where I know Cassian hides, watching us.

The crowd of hunters huddle close and speak to one another in voices that can't be heard.

'What's going on?' Will calls out.

Buzz Cut looks back, his expression more annoyed than ever. 'You and your girlfriend need to move along.'

'Uh, hello? Car trouble,' I remind in an exasperated voice.

Buzz Cut mutters something unintelligible. Hunting draki in front of witnesses isn't their MO, but then that's our plan. To make their job difficult, and give the others time to get away. Except Cassian. He's not going anywhere, apparently.

'We need to move,' the guy holding the box says. 'Before it gets out of range.'

It.

I bristle, fully aware that they're talking about draki. And now I'm certain that little black device spells serious trouble—as if I had any doubts before. Somehow it's a draki tracker. But it's not in high alert around me. Maybe I have to be fully manifested? If that's the case, then the device can only be giving off signals because of Deghan. I almost smirk to think of this small group coming upon Deghan. Yeah. Good luck taking him down.

My half-smirk slips away as a thought strikes me.

I lift a hand to my head and burrow my fingers through my thick mass of hair to the small patch of exposed skin above my ear where they shaved me. Suddenly it all clicks. Cold realization ices down my spine.

119

A lump rises in my throat and I fight to swallow it back down.

I'm pretty certain that if I was to check Miram's head, I would find a similarly shaved spot on her skull. Now I understand what they were trying to do to me right before Will and Cassian rescued me. They were going to implant a tracking device of some sort . . .

The same kind of thing now inside Miram.

My fingers slip away from my scalp and my gaze snaps to the tree line with sudden awareness. They failed on me, but not with Miram. Or Deghan. Not with the amount of time they'd spent as captives. Bile rises in my throat, mingling with an acrid char. I hadn't thought to ask Miram whether she'd been forced under the knife like I had. I'd been too busy focusing on escape, and then, later, coping with Cassian's presumed death.

Urgency swells up inside me now. If Miram or Deghan has been implanted, there is no escape for them. Hunters are all about the pursuit. Bloodhounds. And thanks to the enkros, they've been given the tools to excel at their duty.

Buzz Cut snaps his fingers at us as if we're dogs to be commanded, and I can't help but jump a little, knowing the true danger of that box. 'You two. In the van. Lock the doors.'

Knowing I at least have to stall them, I shake my head and cross my arms firmly across my chest, relieved my voice doesn't shake as I say, 'I don't take orders—'

My words die as he strides across the road towards me with fast steps. Will reaches for my arm, holds me still, communicating that I should keep it together right now even though the prospect of blowing a fireball into this hunter's face not only thrills me—it feels necessary.

The hunter points a long finger at Will. 'Get your girl here in line and get inside that van. We're hunting a dangerous animal and I don't need two dumb kids getting caught in the crossfire.'

Behind him, his team starts removing their gear and weapons from their vehicles. Getting ready to go after the others. I follow their movements with a desperate panic.

My gaze narrows on the box and my fingers curl, nails digging deeply into my palms. I fight down the impulse to snatch it from them and destroy it. Break and shatter it on the ground. They'd know that Will and I aren't the clueless couple with car trouble then. My throat tightens. There has to be a better way . . .

Still, I inch forward, drawn to the box, logic fading as I think only of getting my hands on it, snatching it and destroying it.

Will starts pulling me towards our van. I drag my feet, sending him a pointed look that he ignores.

Once inside the vehicle, closed in the small front space of the van, I burst out with 'The box is a tracking device!'

'I guessed as much,' he answers. Shaking his head as if that weren't his biggest concern, he mutters, 'You're not supposed to be here.'

Out the dirty window, I watch in dread as the hunters disappear into the trees. 'You don't understand. I think the enkros implant some type of homing device in the draki they take captive. In case of escape, you know . . . ' I point to my own head. 'They were about to do it to me. Did you know any of this?' My voice sounds sharper than I intend.

121

Will's expression hardens, the skin around his eyes looking tighter. 'If I knew I would have mentioned it, don't you think, Jacinda?'

I wince, hating that I said that, hating the echo of accusation hovering between us. 'Sorry,' I say sincerely.

Will nods, asking in a brisk tone that lets me know he's moving on, concentrating on coming up with a plan, 'So this device is inside Miram? And Deghan?'

'Yes—I think so.'

'Let's go,' Will spits out. We hop outside, closing the doors softly behind us. I lead the way, stepping silently in a straight line for Cassian's tree.

Looking up, I whisper loudly, 'Come down.'

'I'm right here.'

I spin around with a gasp. My speeding heart lurches. Cassian's behind us, almost fully transformed. His face is entirely draki—sharp angles and hollows, ridged nose, charcoal-toned skin. Only his body isn't there yet. No wings stretch above his shoulders.

'They went this way.' He waves to us.

Will and I share a look and I know I have to try to explain. 'Cassian . . . wait.'

He looks over his shoulder at me without stopping.

I fall in step beside him. 'Miram has a tracking device on her. The enkros put it in her.'

He stops to face me. 'What?'

I sigh, my words tumbling free. 'You heard me. They can find her. Anywhere.'

Panic washes over his face as this sinks in and he starts moving again, growling over his shoulder, 'Why didn't you tell me?'

'I just figured it out,' I say after him.

Cassian's injuries quickly become obvious. He doesn't move with his usual speed and we soon have to slow to stay near him. His breath labours behind us in noisy pants and I know he's pushing himself as much as he can.

The hunters aren't hard to track. Even though they are stealthy, they've torn a path through weeds and brush. Will takes the lead and I place my feet where he steps, one eye on his broad back racing ahead, and the other scanning the green world pulsing around us. Wind sifts through the grass and leaves, but nothing else stirs.

Will stops, holding up a hand. He looks over his shoulder at me, then Cassian. *Be ready,* he mouths. And I know what he means. He's relying on me to use my fire to help save us. He's even relying on Cassian, as injured as he is.

I nod, determined to do what I can with what I am. I'm not letting any of us go back to the enkros . . . or end up as a skin in some hunter's living room. It's not going to happen.

A twig snaps and we freeze. A bird trilling in a nearby tree suddenly stops, its song dying abruptly.

I hear nothing else. Suffocating silence. Too quiet.

My pulse jumps at my neck, rapid and fierce. I look left and right, panic closing in as I brace myself, expecting a hunter to jump out at me at any moment.

When it comes, the scream spills through me like a douse of acid. The sound shudders on the air and my skin flashes prickly hot with recognition. I've heard this scream before. Hear it in my darkest dreams where the past lives.

Cassian knows it, too. 'Miram,' he cries, crashing ahead of us, no longer worried about making noise.

There's no point warning him to take care, to try to keep the element of surprise. Not when his sister is threatened.

I rush to catch up, my thoughts reeling, wondering what's happening, what they're doing to her.

Cassian pulls to a stop ahead, peering through branches as he fights for breath. We arrive behind him. He swings one arm up to keep us from taking a step farther and holds the other one close to his side.

Hunkering low, we watch through the foliage at the scene unfolding. My stomach sinks as if rocks weigh it down when I spot Miram, still in human form, backed up against a tree by a crowd of hunters, her eyes as wild as a cornered animal's.

Cassian growls low in his throat. His rage consumes me, mingling with my fear and panic. Panic fed by the knowledge that her human disguise won't protect her. He wants to break into the midst of them and tear them all apart, each and every one.

I eye the half dozen of them, armed to the teeth, and curl a hand around Cassian's bicep, urging him to stay. His bicep flexes with tension under my fingers. The longing to harm, to destroy, pulses through him. I swallow back a wash of the angry emotion, trying to free myself of his dangerous feelings and inject him with some of my emotion . . . a steady dose of calm that will get him to focus and not do anything stupid.

I look back at Miram and wonder where the others are. My sister and Deghan. I don't blame them for abandoning her, if that's what happened. With a homing mechanism in Miram, it was inevitable the hunters would track her.

I'm just glad Tamra is somewhere safe. I know first-hand that Miram does not hold up well in high-risk situations. I'm rather shocked she hasn't already manifested. As a visiocrypter, even when she manifests she stays the same nude colour, so it's not immediately clear when she begins to shift that she's anything but human. And then I realize it's happening now. I watch as her flesh flashes and shimmers, but she's not totally lost yet.

They surround her like a pack of dogs—shouting at her, at each other, bewildered at the sight of her, a seemingly human girl, and trying to make sense of why they've been led to her when obviously they expected a draki.

It won't take them long to figure it out.

'We don't have much time,' I whisper. We have to do something before they realize who—*what*—they've got cornered. That they didn't make a mistake.

The guy holding the little black box glares at it and shakes it like it might be broken. 'It says we're right on top of it.'

'*It*' again.

Buzz Cut grabs the device from his hands. 'Let me see!' He advances on Miram and waves it over her, sweeping it above her head and down the length of her body. She flinches as if it's a knife poised to stab her.

Even from where we crouch we can hear the beeping become one steady, unrelenting bleep. Buzz Cut lifts it back up to her head and the sound grows even louder.

'What the hell?' He pulls the box away and steps back from Miram, looking from her to the box several times. 'It can't be! She's a girl!'

The hunters erupt all at once in heated conversation.

My body tenses, every muscle stretched tight, ready to spring into the fray. Because there's no choice. I exchange a look with Cassian. Any moment now, they're going to put it together. Unbelievable as it will seem to them, they're about to uncover our greatest secret. Again, we're about to be exposed.

Almost to confirm this, the beeping resumes, blaring loud and unremitting. I glance back to Miram and see that they're holding the locating device over her again. Hovering it just above her head. She swats a hand at it and lets out a small mewl of fear.

'Look at her eyes,' the hunter with the sleek ponytail cries out.

Now they're paying closer attention to her. Noticing all the little signs. Like the pupils of her eyes. Even from where I crouch, I can detect the change in them. The sharp vertical slits, shuddering with her terror.

'She's one of them!'

'But she's a girl!'

'Look at her! Look at her skin—she's not. She's a dragon.'

I struggle free of my clothes, letting them drop at my feet. We lunge forward, but we don't reach Miram. Someone else beats us to her.

Suddenly Tamra is there. Magnificent in full manifest, pale mist flows from her, seeping from every pore. Like an angel, she hangs suspended several feet off the ground, her glistening wings flapping and creating great gusts of wind, spinning leaves and other small debris on the air.

Pride swells in me—to see what Tamra is, what she's become, and in so short a time. She really is this beautiful, powerful, wondrous thing.

126

The hunters cry out, shouting orders as they scramble for their weapons. Even as mind-numbing mist pours from Tamra's body, I see that it's not happening fast enough. It won't take out the hunters in time. Not before they begin shooting.

Cassian realizes this, too. He sweeps in and snatches hold of Miram, getting her out of there while everyone's attention is still fixed on Tamra.

I step out into the open, shouting to distract them from shooting Tamra. I get my wish. Their attention swings to me. Will plunges into the fray, yanking me out of the way just as a tranq dart whizzes past me.

I regain my feet and watch in horror as a hunter lifts a crossbow, aiming directly for Tamra's chest.

'No!' I dive through the air. Wind surges around me as I cut directly in front of Tamra. My lungs contract and swell. The heat rushes through me and explodes out on a breath.

Orange-blue flames scorch the hunter before he can squeeze the trigger. The shape of him is there, a dark smudge, a blurred figure lost inside a burst of fire.

His screams claw my ears as crackling flames engulf him. I touch down on the ground, frozen. My blood curdles in my veins, disgusted at the sight of what I've done. The other hunters surround him, stripping off their jackets and pushing him down on the ground, shouting at him to roll as they attempt to beat out the flames devouring the man. The smell of roasting flesh fills the air.

I did this.

The mist swirls thicker than ever, and the hunters' movements grow slow, sluggish, as one by one they start to fall, dropping into deep sleep.

'Jacinda!' I look up. Will jumps over a fallen hunter and grabs me by both arms, giving me a small shake. 'Are you OK?'

I snap from my daze and look away from all the fallen hunters. The odour of charred flesh still chokes me. OK? No. I'm *not* OK. Tamra's eyes close and her head rolls almost drunkenly on her shoulders.

I catch movement to my left and spin, ready to release my fire again even though I'm stunned at the damage I wreaked. Despite what that hunter would have gladly done to Tamra, to me, I'm shaken that I could have killed him.

But it's no hunter standing there. It's Deghan, watching us with bemusement in his slate eyes. He scans us, his attention lingering on my sister. Tamra takes an unsteady step and he's there, catching her when her legs give out from under her. He lifts her up against his chest. She closes her eyes and presses fingers to her temples as though her head pains her.

His gaze locks with mine. I give a single nod, accepting that he's got her. He'll keep her safe.

My gaze sweeps through the mist, measuring each of the fallen hunters, lingering on the one with smoking burns on his arms. I motion to him, knowing that without treatment, left here unconscious, he might not survive.

Cassian is there again, Miram close to his side. He shakes his head at me. 'We have to go. There are probably others, waiting for them to report in.'

'I won't leave him to die.'

'He would have killed us—'

'I don't care!' I look at Will and see he's staring at

the smoking body, too. Will's eyes look distant, oddly glazed . . . and I can't help thinking if he's wondering about his family. That his father or Xander could be lying there. That I could have burned any of them had they been the ones to track us. That it could still happen. Is he sickened at what I did? As sickened as I am . . .

Will's lips barely move when he speaks. 'We can't leave him to die here.' Relief washes through me that he's with me in this.

Cassian snorts, his dark eyes flashing annoyance. 'Of course you would say that.'

'Why don't we call nine-one-one?' Tamra offers, blinking as though fighting to regain control of herself. She motions for Deghan to set her down. He carefully releases her, one hand still on her arm in case she should lose her balance again. 'Leave an anonymous tip. An ambulance will come.'

Will and I share a look. I nod. 'OK.'

'Good,' Cassian declares. 'Now let's get moving.'

My chest tightens. I massage there, right in the centre, as if I can rub out the feeling. Useless. I doubt it will ever go away. That I'll ever feel normal again. Normal for me, anyway.

I may have killed a man. Knowing I did it to save my sister doesn't make it any easier to accept. Suddenly I'm not sure what I should do any more. What's right. What's wrong. Every direction I look, I see pain. I send a sidelong glance to Will. His features are intense, like something carved from stone.

With a grim nod, I follow, plunging back into the woods. But I don't feel relief. I don't feel free. My chest feels heavy, weighed down . . . with every step, every mile, that burden only gets heavier. This journey feels . . . endless.

When we reach the van we stop, our breaths ragged, but I think it's more from the emotion and tumult of everything that just happened than from our actual sprint.

Will's face is stoic, his square jaw locked as he opens the door for us and stands there, blocking us from getting inside. 'Before we go anywhere we need to talk, get a few things straight.'

I nod. The rules of the game have changed.

Tamra glances around us uneasily as if more hunters might appear. The trees climb to the sky, blocking out the afternoon sun and shrouding us in long shadows.

Will arches an eyebrow at me. I nod dully. He's right, of course. It's on me to explain. I'm the one that figured out about the homing device in Miram.

'The hunters are going to track us again.' I swallow and cut my gaze to Miram, amending, '*You*. They're going to find you again.' I look at Deghan, wondering if he knows what I'm talking about and just hasn't bothered to tell us.

'And you, too. Wherever you go, they'll track you. Both of you. You can't lose them.'

'How'd this happen?' Cassian demands, his eyes brightly feral, pupils quivering with emotion as he grapples with the knowledge that his sister isn't free. Not yet.

'The enkros plant tracking devices in the heads of their captives.' I reflexively brush my fingers over my own pale patch of flesh hiding in my hair. I nod in the direction of Miram. 'That's how the hunters were led straight to her.'

Will watches me intently, missing nothing—including the way I rub at my head. They'd come so close to putting their mark on me—inside me.

'Did they do it to you?' Cassian asks.

I shake my head, dropping my hand. 'No. You stopped them right before they could do it.'

'You were lucky,' Deghan says in his rumbling draki speech.

'And you?' Cassian's head whips in his direction. 'You were there a long time. They implanted you with the chip, too.'

'They could never get close enough to me to do it.' He glances down at his steel-coloured flesh. 'Anyone who did . . . ' His voice fades, but I understand.

'They never knocked you out with one of their tranq guns?' Cassian asks.

'When they tried, they couldn't break my skin.' He taps himself. 'Good as armour.'

Suddenly, I have a good idea of why he survived so long with them—why he lived when all the others in his pride perished. They could never touch him.

Cassian drags his hands through his hair and paces a short invisible line, pausing only to stare in misery at his sister a few feet away, gazing off into the thick press of trees. She has to have heard what we've said, but she shows no reaction. She hasn't stopped shaking since she found herself surrounded by hunters. Since she learned what's inside her. She'll never be free until we figure out a way to remove it. I'd probably be shaking, too. My fingers move to that shaved spot on my

131

head again. Maybe worse. I might be clawing that thing out myself.

'What do we do?' Cassian swings around to look at each of us. This is the moment when I could—*should*—say, *What do you mean* we?

I say nothing. Only *think* agonizing, gnawing thoughts. I'm supposed to be leaving, walking away from all of this. I did what I promised and got Miram out of the stronghold. This should be the end of it.

I feel Will's stare on the side of my face and know that's what he's thinking, too. That we're supposed to be free of the pride. Right now. Freedom is close, almost ours—if I'll only take it.

Cassian's gaze cuts into me, and worse than that penetrating stare are the waves of absolute helplessness rushing from him to me like a raging, swollen river. His need and desperation mingle with my own emotions . . . overcome them, drown them until they're just a whispery echo. I can't ignore them. I can't ignore *him*.

He shakes his head again. 'We can't go digging around in her head to get this . . . *thing* out of her. We could kill her doing that.'

I nod slowly. 'I know. You have to take her home, talk to the others.' As much as I distrust Severin and many of the elders, they've been around longer than any of us. They know things. Especially Nidia. Maybe they've faced something like this before. 'Maybe Nidia or one of the verda will know what to do,' I suggest.

I can't think of a better solution. It's not like we can admit Miram to a local hospital and ask them to remove the implant. I gnaw on the edge of my thumb. My mum would have had ideas, I'm sure. She could have removed the chip without killing the patient.

This only reminds me that she's gone. That *they* banished her. I bite down a little harder on the salty edge of my thumb, welcoming the stab of pain. I can't think about that betrayal right now. It will only make me angry and cloud my thoughts, and I need a cool head right now.

'You want to take her home?' Tamra leans closer to Deghan, and I wonder if she's conscious of the action. 'Back to the pride where the hunters can follow? How is that smart?'

'Not directly to the township. Miram can hide somewhere nearby . . . on the mountain,' I say, thinking fast. 'If hunters track her to that area, it's not that great a risk. They already know draki are in the vicinity.'

I'm referring to Will's family, of course.

Will stares at me, his gaze unreadable, and I wonder what he's thinking. At least with Cassian I know his emotions. That's what happens when you experience each and every feeling together. And then, just as suddenly as I have this thought, I feel bad for comparing the two of them. For wishing my relationship with Will to be anything like what I have with Cassian. Will and I are real. What Cassian and I have is a manipulation, a result of bonding. Nothing more.

Cassian nods. 'Yes. That will work.' He approaches his sister and squeezes her shoulder tenderly. She looks up at him, finally showing that she's paying attention. 'You'll be fine, Miram. We'll go home . . . we're going to fix this.'

She nods and leans into him. He puts an arm around her shoulder and strokes a hand over her sandy brown hair, petting her like she's a child. And I realize that she pretty much is. Older than Lia, but not tougher. At the thought of Lia I wince. Could a hunter already have caught her? What about the rest of the freed draki? Roc and the others? Were they already captured? Or worse?

I exhale a heavy breath. I can't worry about them, too. We have our own problem to deal with. Miram in Cassian's arms fills me with such desolation . . . It's impossible to remain unaffected. To *not* care. Especially with Cassian's emotions bombarding me. Rage. Defeat. Fear and sorrow.

'All right. We can't stay here.' Will's voice jars me back to reality. I tear my gaze from Cassian and Miram. His expression is so knowing, and I flush guiltily, my skin prickling hotly. I hate that I have this bond with Cassian that forever links us. That it's something Will and I can never have. If I have this bond with anyone, it *should* be Will. But that's not possible. It never was.

'Let's get moving.'

We all pile in again. I ride up front with Will this time. It's a relief not to face the others, especially Miram. There's too much pain and regret when I look at her and think about what the enkros did. She's still a captive even if she's with us.

We bump along the rutted road, dirt billowing around us as we head back to the highway. Will reaches across the space separating us and takes my hand. I release a breath I didn't realize I was holding. My fingers tighten around his hand and squeeze hard, needing him so much it's a physical pang in my chest. The fear of losing him has always nipped at me, a growling beast snapping at my heels. But now it coats my mouth in a sour, metallic film. And I know why.

I'm considering helping Cassian and Miram return to the pride. And I might lose him if I do.

CHAPTER FIFTEEN

Will and I say nothing. It's as though we know once we start talking, things will be said that will change everything. Change us. The dreams we had for ourselves aren't as close to coming true as we thought. He has to know that. Sense that. For now, silence is my only comfort.

Although in that quiet, my mind circles back to the terrible thing I've done, to the possibility that I killed someone. We did stop to place a call to 911, but the awful feelings still nag at me. A tightness builds inside me that makes every breath an agonizing struggle for air. Words are beyond me. But even without words, my thoughts are loud inside my head. And I have plenty more to consider. There's the matter of Miram. As long as she's with us, as long as the homing device stays inside her . . . I shake my head. We'll never be safe. It's a situation I can't ignore. I can't let them all go on their merry way back to the pride as if this weren't a problem.

We travel over an hour before Will slows the van. I blink like I'm waking from a dream as he pulls over at one of those mega travel centres that boasts multiple restaurants and showers. It's practically a small city. The prospect of clean hair and fresh clothes perks me up a bit. Will parks at the far edge of the lot where there aren't any other vehicles.

I join Will as he opens the back door. Everyone looks drained, slumped low, adrenaline long spent. Cassian clutches his side as though his ribs still pain him. He probably hurt himself again in the mad dash to rescue his sister. Tamra twists a matted lock of hair between her fingers.

'Anyone want a shower?' I ask, forcing a ring of cheerfulness into my voice.

Tamra is the quickest. Grabbing our bags, she hops down, equally delighted. Cassian follows. Miram doesn't move.

'Miram,' I say gently, looking at her where she huddles in the corner with her knees pulled to her chest, her expression uncertain, like she isn't sure if she can come or not. And who can blame her? 'Would you like to wash up, too? You can wear some of our clothes.'

She doesn't respond.

Cassian prompts her. 'Miram?'

She gives a small jerk and then nods once, scooting towards the van door. 'Yeah. Thanks,' she whispers, dropping down. Cassian drapes an arm around her and pulls her close. She forces a watery smile and snuggles into the shelter of his body. His face fixes in a cringe, but he doesn't complain or remind her of his injuries.

Tamra lingers at the door, peering back in at Deghan. He sits with his wrists propped on his knees. 'You going to be OK?' she asks.

I pat her shoulder and stifle a sigh. 'C'mon. I'm pretty sure he can handle himself, Tamra.'

Her pale cheeks pink up, and she nods. Will shuts the van door, and we all walk together to the facility, guys and girls parting when we reach the showering area. I let Tamra and Miram go first. There are enough showers, but with Miram acting as a giant homing device for hunters . . . well, someone should stand guard.

Miram emerges with a towel around her. Her uncertainty returns when she sees me. I smile encouragingly, hoping to reassure her. Her expression eases, softens. I hand her some clothes and wait while she changes. She resurfaces in the fresh clothes, rubbing her hair dry with the towel.

'You can go ahead.' She gestures to the shower stall.

'That's OK.' Tamra's still showering. I can't leave her alone yet.

'Oh.' She nods as my reason for staying sinks in. Squaring off in front of the mirror, she lifts my hairbrush to begin untangling her hair and stops, the brush hovering mid-air, directly above her head. I understand at once, following her gaze to where it's fixed—to the incision behind her ear.

I gently remove the brush from her clenched fingers.

'Here. Let me.' She stares at me, looking almost startled to see me.

I begin brushing. The fine sandy-coloured strands untangle easily. I look over the top of her head, meeting her eyes as she watches me in the mirror. It's silent, save for the distant noise of showers.

I start at the sound of her voice. 'I should have gone with you.'

138

I pause for a moment, then resume brushing. 'What do you mean?'

'When you tried to get me to leave with you and Will . . . I should have gone. I was just so *used* to not liking you. I didn't want to follow you.'

'It's OK.' What else can I say? It's over and done.

'None of this would be happening if I had gone with you. I'm sorry. For everything, Jacinda.'

I shrug, trying to act like it's nothing. 'Then we never would have found Deghan. Some good came of it. He'd still be a prisoner in there. All those other draki would still be captives.' True, all the draki had implants, and are most likely going to be captured again, but they at least have a chance now. Just like Miram does. And I don't want her focusing on the negatives.

'I guess I should care about them,' she says, looking at her scrubbed-fresh face in the mirror. Impossibly young, innocent. 'But I just wish none of it had ever happened. I wish I were home. With Dad. Aunt Jabel.'

I finish with her hair, unsure what to say to that. Not sure there is anything to say.

Tamra joins us then, already dressed. 'Your turn,' she says.

'Great. I'll be fast. Why don't you two go get some food and I'll meet you back at the van?'

Tamra nods and gathers up her things. I shower quickly, even though I would love nothing more than to stand under the warm spray for an hour and let it ease all the tension from my body.

I meet up with Will on the way back from the shower. He's carrying a brown paper bag.

'Get anything good?'

'Oh yeah.' He smiles. Now that he's freshly showered and shaved, his clean soapy scent fills my nose. 'C'mon. I'll show you.' Taking my hand, he pulls me off the asphalt parking lot to one of the many picnic tables dotting the grass.

We sit on top of a splintery-wood table and he fumbles inside the brown bag. I try to get a glimpse, but he shakes a finger at me and twists his body so I can't see inside it.

He looks over his shoulder. 'Ready?'

I grin and bounce my knees. 'Yes! Show me.'

He whips around. 'Ta-da!'

I stare down uncomprehendingly at the box in his hands. 'What is it?'

He looks from me to the box in amazement. *'What is it?'* he echoes. 'You don't know?'

I read the print on the box. 'Cracker Jack?'

He nods excitedly.

I examine the box. Caramel-coated popcorn and peanuts. 'So . . . junk food?'

He looks appalled. 'Not just any junk food. It's like the first junk food ever.' He rips open the box and shakes some of the sticky popcorn into my palm, then his. 'This was my mum's favourite.'

He tosses the snack into his mouth and chews. I watch for a moment, enjoying the sight of him, the way his eyes crinkle in pleasure. I relish just sitting here. With him. 'You don't talk about her that much.'

'I was so young when she died. I wish I could remember her more clearly,' he says matter-of-factly as he shakes some more Cracker Jack into his hand. 'At night, in my bed, I try to run through all the memories of her

140

I do have, almost like I'm exercising them, you know?'
He looks at me. 'Keeping them fresh and in shape before
they fade away completely.'

I nod and blink suddenly burning eyes. 'Yeah. I get
that.' Haven't I done the same thing with my own memories of my father?

His gaze roves over my face—like he's memorizing
me and this moment. 'Yeah. I guess you do.'

Tossing back his head, he drops more Cracker Jack
into his mouth.

I copy him. 'Hmm, pretty good.'

He shakes his head and bumps me with his shoulder.
'I can't believe you've never had Cracker Jack before.'

My eyes widen. 'Had it? I've never even seen the stuff,'
I confess.

'Oh, blasphemy.'

'Hey! I've spent like . . . what? Two months out in the
human world? My education hasn't covered Cracker Jack
yet.' I giggle, swaying on the top of the table. 'I've got a
lot to learn. I admit it.'

Still wearing that melting grin, he reaches for my hair,
smoothing a hand down the wet strands. 'We'll have all
the time in the world. And I'll teach you,' he murmurs.
And suddenly I'm fairly certain we're not talking about
future lessons in junk food.

My cheeks burn as he leans in to kiss me. At my lips,
he whispers, 'Soon, Jacinda. It will be us. We're going to
have peace. We'll be free. And happy.'

Every part of me comes alive at the first brush of his
mouth. I taste the salty Cracker Jack on his mouth and
know I'll never forget the sensation of this moment.

'We better get going,' I say, standing.

'Yeah.' He sighs, grabbing the bag. 'But wait. Almost forgot the best part.' He shakes popcorn everywhere, digging through the box. 'Ah, I got it!'

'What is that?'

'The prize. Every box comes with a prize.' Something falls into his palm. He gazes at it for a long moment, a slow smile curving his well-carved lips.

'What?' I nudge him with my elbow playfully.

He seizes my hand. 'This is perfect. Until I can get you something better.' He slides a purple plastic ring on my finger. The band fits just right.

We both stare at it for a moment. The top of the plastic band is a hollowed-out heart. I outline that tiny heart with one fingertip.

'Now you can look down at your hand any time. Even if I'm not there, you'll know.' His warm fingers squeeze mine, and our gazes find each other.

'Know what?' I whisper.

'That you have my heart. That I love you.'

Those words, his deep gaze . . . I can't catch my breath. But then I feel as though something like oxygen might not be necessary when I have him. He feeds me . . . breathes life into me. Makes everything good. He stuck with me through everything: my disappearance, my bonding with Cassian . . . always putting me above himself. It's a miracle he hasn't run in the opposite direction.

In the distance, the van honks. I look up and spot Tamra standing near the driver's side, sliding her arm back out the window. She's anxious to get moving—no doubt nervous about the hunters catching up to us. At this reminder, the smile slips from my face. Just like that, the happy moment is diminished.

'C'mon.' I head towards the van. I only get a few feet before Will reclaims my hand. And I'm glad for that. Glad at the feel of his finger tracing the ring band on my hand. That no matter how bad everything is he hasn't let go of me. Maybe he never will. No matter what comes. No matter what I ask of him. I don't know what I ever did to deserve him. I just know that I don't want to lose this boy who has come to mean so much to me. Everything.

'Oh, hey. I forgot to get batteries for the flashlights and lamps. I think we're low.' He thrusts the bag of food into my arms. 'I'll be right back.'

I turn, admire his lean form as he jogs back to the megacomplex.

'Jacinda?'

I start at the sound of my name. Cassian stands behind me. I'm not surprised I didn't hear his approach . . . but I am surprised I didn't *feel* him there. Annoyance flickers in his gaze as he looks beyond me to Will. Looking back at me, he quickly cools the emotion from his eyes, but I still feel its lingering touch inside.

'Yes?' I ask, hating the awkwardness of the moment.

'I just wanted to thank you.'

'For what?'

'For everything you've done for my sister. I know you two haven't always gotten along.'

I smile. 'How about never?'

He smiles back, angling his head in agreement. And in that killer smile, the flash of his straight, white teeth in his swarthy face, I'm reminded just how many girls covet this boy. And not just for his power and position in the pride. 'Yeah. She hasn't made it easy for you to like

143

her. Afraid my father had a lot to do with that.' His smile fades. 'But you still wanted to rescue her . . . and stood by her when you thought I was dead.'

'I did it for you.'

Quiet falls between us and I fidget nervously beneath his intent stare. I think about his words . . . how we risked so much to rescue her . . . and swallow tightly. She is still in peril. She isn't out of the woods yet. Was he trying to guilt me into staying and helping? But looking into his liquid dark eyes, I see only sincerity in the lines of his face. There is no ulterior motive in this conversation.

'Here.' He takes the bag from my arms and together we walk towards the van, our steps silent on the asphalt.

I send him a measuring glance. There's a slight limp in his tread. 'How are you doing?'

'I'll live. Should be my old self soon. We heal quickly, after all.' True. Which makes me think that he must have been hurt very bad to still suffer the effects. Something curls up and withers inside me to think of Cassian in pain.

He shoots me a look, his lips twisting into a smile that I imagine is supposed to encourage me and convince me of his well-being. 'Don't beat yourself up, Jacinda.' Of course he would *feel* my feelings—that the idea of him hurt nauseates me. 'It's over and done. I'll be OK,' he says, gently stroking a finger down my cheek. He frowns, stepping back and dropping his hand. Regret over the touch swiftly slides through him. We reach the van and he conveniently moves away, carrying the bag to the front seat.

I stand beside the back doors, the rumble of his words replaying through my head. *It's over.* Is it? Is it really? Can

144

I let go of him and the others with that question, that fear winding through me like a virus?

I rest my head against the hard wall of the van and blow out a great gust of breath. A dull headache throbs behind my eyes. Cassian wanted to ride up front. I thought the request strange but didn't think a little alone time between Will and Cassian was a bad thing.

I rub my eyelids with my thumb and forefinger, pressing upward into the bridge of my nose. I do this several times, trying to ease my headache.

Deghan sits across from me, just staring with his pewter eyes . . . eyes so cold I shiver. Finally, I can't stand it any more. I drop my hand from my eyes and demand, 'What are you looking at?'

'You.'

I snort. 'Clearly. Why do you keep staring at me?'

Tamra looks up, evidently interested in his response.

He makes a small motion with his hand. 'You remind me of someone.'

Shaking my head, I glance away, down at the van floor, feeling its rumble through the soles of my shoes. I'm not interested in some draki that I remind him of, some draki who he—

My gaze snaps back to him. Every nerve in my body pulls taut, suddenly alert.

'Who?' I demand.

He shrugs. 'Just another captive. He was there when I was brought in. He was an onyx but you remind me of him. The way you rub at your eyes and nose. He did that. Also the way you hold yourself . . . angle your head to the side when someone is talking. You get this intent look on your face. Like you're almost angry.'

Was? It's the word that ricochets through my head.

He continues, 'You have the same . . . way about you.'

I'm shaking now. A sick feeling churns in my stomach. 'What happened to him?'

'They took him out of his cell one day for more experimenting.' A dullness enters his eyes. 'He never came back. But you know the worst thing about it?'

Worse than his dying?

'What?' Tamra asks, holding herself as still as stone, and I know the same thoughts whir through her mind.

'His own kind betrayed him. He said someone in his pride tricked him into getting captured. Led him right into the path of hunters.'

My skin flashes hot and cold at this. I fight to swallow around the lump in my throat. 'What was his name?' I say tightly, my lips numb, barely moving.

Don't say my father's name. Not Magnus. Not Magnus.

'Magnus.'

I vault to my feet, arms wide, stretching out at my sides as if seeking a handhold, something to cling to. My world spins. Red fills my vision. Tamra lowers her head into her hands and surrenders to body-shaking tears.

I pound on the van wall until my palms sting, and even then I don't quit. 'Stop,' I shout. 'Stop!'

The van slows. Once it stops, I fling open the doors and run—take off through the trees running as fast and hard as I can. Not caring where I'm going. Just trying to get away, escape the pain, the throbbing, unrelenting ache in my chest.

In the distance, I hear my name being shouted, but I don't turn back. I don't stop.

I run, flying through the trees. But the pain doesn't fade. I can't leave it behind. It follows me still. And in a fresh surge of anguish I realize it always will.

I stop, silent tears streaming hot tracks down my cheeks. I sway for a moment before I drop, land on my knees. With a keening sob, I bow at the waist and retch, emptying the contents of my stomach. When there's nothing left inside me, I curl into a tight ball on the ground. Twigs and pine needles scratch at every exposed inch of me, but I don't have the energy to care.

Now I know. I finally know. After all this time. Dad is dead. Betrayed by someone from the pride. Someone I've lived with for years.

Leaves rustle near me as Tamra steps into view, like a wraith materializing from nothing. Her chest heaves from her race through the woods. Her hair floats in a wild nimbus of silvery white around her. Our gazes lock as we share in the knowledge, the truth of what happened to Dad. Her frosty gaze gleams wet across the few feet separating us.

'Tamra,' I whisper, her name crumbling from me.

Her face is stricken, the perfect reflection of what I'm feeling. She nods jerkily, words unnecessary between us. We're living the same nightmare right now.

In an instant we're hugging each other. Weeping like little girls. I wipe at my runny nose.

'I guess I always hoped he might be alive,' I say between sobbing gasps.

'I know. Me too.' She nods doggedly. 'Mum. I want Mum.' Her voice breaks and she's crying again.

I grip her shoulders, determination stealing over me. 'We're going to find her.' She's the only parent we have left. Now with the truth of Dad's fate choking me, I feel Mum's void all the more keenly.

A branch snaps. We both turn to see Will. He stops, holding up a hand as if to apologize for intruding.

'It's OK.' Tamra sniffs, and wipes at her wet cheeks. 'I—I need a moment alone.'

'You don't have to—' Will starts to say, but she shakes her head and slips past him.

I stare up at Will, feeling raw and exposed, broken. Like I'll never be whole again.

Then he's there, pulling me into his arms. I sag against him, let him support me. He sighs my name. 'Jacinda.'

I grip his shirt tightly, my fingers bloodless as they squeeze. 'He's really gone,' I say, looking into his ever-changing eyes.

'I know, I know,' he croons.

'I always wanted the truth . . . but deep down I believed he was alive. I realize that now. All this time—I never thought he was really gone.'

'It's better you know. No more wondering and uselessly guessing.'

The tears roll down my cheeks. I'm convinced there's nothing *better* about this. Before I had hope. Now I have nothing. Nothing but grief in the absolute certainty that Dad is dead. I'll never see him again.

If possible, I hold on to Will even tighter. As if that can somehow ease this gnawing pain. But the pain only grows. Blossoms in my chest until an emotion even more powerful takes over. Fury swells inside me as new, ugly thoughts push their way into my head. And I let it—I let the fury take over.

I drag a burning breath deep inside where it only grows hotter. Someone betrayed my father, and it doesn't take long to conclude who that someone probably was. *Severin.* Corbin had plainly conveyed his uncle's animosity toward my father—how threatened Severin felt by my father. But Dad hadn't been trying to take over. He just wanted to take his family elsewhere, away from the pride. Too bad we didn't escape before he was led into a trap.

I exhale through my nose, flexing my clenched fingers, loosening their grip on Will, not needing to hang on so tightly any more, as new purpose fills me. I know what I have to do. I'm going back. Back to the pride.

Before I sought truth. Now I seek justice.

Only when I find it, when the traitor is revealed and punished for what he did to Dad, can I heal. Then I'll be free.

CHAPTER SIXTEEN

Little has been said since my return to the van with Will. We all sit shell-shocked in the back, numb expressions on our faces. My stomach rolls sickly. First the encounter with the hunters, then learning that Miram is a ticking time bomb, and then the news about Dad. What's next? I feel the van shudder to a stop as if it, too, is exhausted.

We have finally reached the truck stop where we left Will's Land Rover. This is where Will and Tamra and I are supposed to at last part ways with Cassian and Miram. This is when I finally leave the pride behind me.

Only I can't do that.

I should know by now that nothing is as simple as I expect. Even if I didn't know the truth about Dad, there's still Miram. Something has to be done about her tracking implant. Although she's Severin's daughter, and even worked for him, spying on me, I'm not going to take it out on her.

I take a pained blink. Is this ever going to get easy? Ever not be so . . . hard?

Stepping out, I glance around at our new surroundings. We're parked behind a deserted gas station, which blocks us from view of the road and the cars that whip past. I shift where I stand. Loose asphalt crumbles beneath my shoes, weeds growing between the uneven cracks. Will's Land Rover sits close by, right where we left it.

The van doors remain open, but Deghan stays hidden within. Tamra emerges, but hovers close to the doors, her body angled toward the hulking grey draki, whose eyes never leave her. A strange, unspoken bond has formed between them since our encounter with the hunters. It's like they're linked by some invisible cord.

I roll my eyes. Now isn't the time for Tamra to develop some kind of puppy-love infatuation with a draki who can't even access his human side any more. This strikes me as especially ironic since not that long ago Tamra was unable to access her draki self.

'What now?' she asks me, even as her gaze drifts toward Deghan.

I look pointedly at him. 'He has to go to the pride. Like Cassian said.'

Tamra's lips flatten into a thin line. I know her expressions well. She's grown even more attached to Deghan than I realized if the idea of leaving him bothers her this much. She looks on the verge of saying something when Will speaks.

'Well,' Will announces. 'I guess this is goodbye.' Nothing can hide the eager light from his eyes. He's waited a long time for this. We both have.

But I can't ignore the tiny flare of panic flickering inside my chest. *This is it.* I have to break it to him now.

'I suppose so.' Cassian nods brusquely, revealing none of his regret at parting ways with us. With *me*. But I feel it anyway—a stinging burn behind my eyes. 'We'll take the van. The hunters should have no memory of it, thanks to Tamra.'

Thanks to Tamra the hunters shouldn't remember *us*. Period.

I glance at Miram. She's moved a small distance from the rest of us. She hugs herself and stares into the distant tree line, and I wonder at her thoughts.

Will's voice comes from beside me. 'Ready?'

Turning, I meet his gaze and stare at him a long time. Long enough for him to know something's wrong, long enough for a wariness to fall over his face.

His eyes sharpen. 'Jacinda?'

I shrug feebly, and hold up a hand in supplication, willing him to understand what I'm about to say. And all I see at that moment is the purple plastic ring on my finger. It mocks me as the words spill from my lips: 'We can't just let them go back by themselves. Cassian still isn't a hundred per cent. What if they're tracked down by hunters before reaching the pride?'

And there's more. More I can't admit aloud yet. I want to avenge my father. I want everyone to know what happened to him. I want my father's killer brought to justice. My hands curl tightly at my sides, opening and closing. Cassian shoots me a curious look and I force my hands to still.

As the first draki to break into an enkros stronghold I'll have credibility. I helped rescue Miram . . . and another draki—a witness to my father's death. Deghan is all the proof I need. The pride will listen and then it'll be Severin's turn to stand trial before everyone—exposed for his crimes. My pulse skitters in anticipation at the prospect.

Cassian looks between me and Will, his eyes suddenly bright. I feel his hope. It swells through me in a giddy, bubbling rush.

'Come with me, Will. See this thing through with me.' I watch him. I wait, breathless, my chest unbearably tight with the notion that he'll refuse. That he won't want to come with me. That he'll hear my words and turn away from me. My thumb rolls the plastic band of the ring. 'I know it's a lot to ask . . . ' I drop my gaze to my hands. 'I understand if you can't come with me . . .' *But it will break my heart.*

He storms away without a word. Something shudders inside me as I watch his retreat. He doesn't move to the van, instead marches past the dilapidated building. I shoot everyone a quick glance and then follow, running after him. 'Will! Will, wait!'

He rounds the building's side. As he passes an old vending machine, he turns and sends his fist into the ancient, stained plastic front. The yellowed plastic shatters into tiny pieces everywhere.

I stop, panting less from my short run and more from my anxiousness to reach him. He braces both hands on each side of the old machine with his head bowed, neck muscles straining with tension.

I wet my lips and glance behind me to make sure no one has followed. 'Will?' I've never seen him this angry . . . this unrestrained. I'm not sure what to say. 'Are you OK?'

He looks up sharply, levelling me with eyes bright with fury. 'Am I OK?'

I resist the urge to step back, instead just nod.

'Are you kidding?' The sound of his voice cuts me. He's not the Will I know right then. Dirt stirs at my feet, curling tufts of earth, and I know it's his doing, his anger affecting the very ground we stand on. 'I'm starting to think we're never going to be together, Jacinda.'

'Don't say that.'

He waves a hand. 'You don't want to let any of it go. Not even for me.'

'That's not true.'

'No?' He angles his head as he studies me. 'Can you tell me that you'll ever be able to let it go? The pride? Cassian?'

'Yes,' I say, glad to hear that my voice is strong and steady. 'I will. We just have to do this one thing—'

'Going back to the pride is no small thing. Especially for you.' He swallows and I watch the cords of his throat work. 'And me.'

I exhale and nod, a sinking feeling starting in my stomach. I'm asking a lot. Too much. 'I can't expect this of you. You're right.' I bite into my lip, withering inside at what this means. 'By now Corbin would have told them all about you.'

A stillness comes over him. 'So what are you saying?'

What am I saying?

I swallow. 'We can part ways. Temporarily, of course,' I quickly say. 'We'll meet later—'

He comes alive again. His hands close around my arms. 'No. Not again. I'm not leaving you again, Jacinda. Not to face this alone.'

Relief ripples through me. But I push it away.

'No, you're right,' I say, determined to keep him safe, but no less determined to see this through and get justice. 'The risk for you is too great—'

He shakes his head fiercely, his eyes glinting. 'We're doing this.' He slides one hand along my face, his palm cupping my cheek. 'And then we'll see if you come up with another reason to keep us from being together. Then I'll know.'

I shake my head. 'It's not like that—'

'Really? It's not? You don't feel bound to the pride? To Cassian?' He holds my gaze, unblinking.

Silence stretches. I wet my lips. 'That's not why . . .'

'Then what?' he asks, his eyes soft and melting as they delve into me. The plea there is something I can't deny. Unable to stop myself, I lean into his hand, revel in the sensation of his skin against mine, the rasp of his calluses on the curve of my face.

'My father—' I stop as the look in his eyes sharpens with understanding.

My voice drops in a fervent, rushed whisper. The pain of my father's death, his betrayal, stabs through me again with a sudden fierceness. I doubt it will ever go away. It will always be there, ready to greet me first thing every morning. But if I can achieve some retribution, perhaps it will soften the edges of the pain, make it more manageable. 'I can't let that go yet.'

'Will you ever, Jacinda? What if you don't get the justice you want? How long can we do this? How long do we keep getting dragged back into the web of a life you claim to want no part of?'

'I've got to try. I'll tell you when it's over.' I wish I could give him a less lame answer than that, but it's too complicated for anything else.

'You'll tell me?' He arches an eyebrow.

'Yes.' I hold my breath, unsure of his response.

He smiles then. A crooked, self-deprecating little smile that makes my belly twist. 'OK, Jacinda. I'm in.'

He takes my hand and pulls me along. Something loosens and flutters inside me. I'm sure in a way I've never felt before. I know where it is I'm supposed to be. Forever and always. Whether I live among the pride—a new pride, changed for the better once Severin is deposed, or out in the human world—or maybe somehow straddling both worlds, I'm meant to be with Will. Us. That's what I've been fighting for . . . and somewhere along the way I forgot that, too busy battling for other things: my draki, Mum, Tamra, Dad, Miram.

'Agreed?' He stops before we round the building, his hazel gaze fastened on me.

I nod. And I realize I'm both my strongest and weakest with him. And I guess that's love. When you're at your most vulnerable.

'I love you,' I say suddenly.

He blinks as though the words surprise him. Haven't I told him that before? I thought I had . . . back in Chaparral, when I had to leave him. But I was in draki form then. He couldn't have understood. Taking his face in both my hands, I stand on tiptoes. 'I love you,' I repeat before I press my mouth to his, kissing him long and slow.

He hesitates only a moment before pulling me closer, tighter against him. Desperation burns between us. His hands move from my hair, to my arms, and my back.

156

Roaming, touching me everywhere. As if I might disappear from him in the flash of a second. He spins me until my back is pressed against the brick wall. His mouth, my mouth . . . there is no distinction . . .

There's only need.

He breaks away, his serrated breath a hot fan in my ear, thrilling me and spiking my pulse faster. His deep voice fills my ear. 'We better get a move on.'

Reluctant, I nod and step back.

He looks over my shoulder as if he can see around the corner to the others. 'With that homing device on Miram, hunters will be coming. It's only a matter of time.'

Only a matter of time.

'Yeah. Of course.' Turning, I lead the way back to the van, still holding Will's hand and trying to shake off the flicker of unease in my heart that this might be a mistake. I have to believe that returning to the pride with Will at my side is the right thing to do. The right choice.

CHAPTER SEVENTEEN

Back home, on the mountain, on the ground that I know so well, I feel restored, heartened. A low mist drifts over lush grasses that brush my legs as we walk through thick foliage where no path exists. Cassian's the only one who might know this mountain better than I do. We proceed carefully. Aside from our fellow draki who could be lurking in the trees, trying to decide what to make of our motley group, hunters can't be far behind us. Cassian leads the way, his gait a little livelier, his injuries less evident, and I suspect just being back here has rejuvenated him as well.

We follow as he guides us somewhere to wait—hidden from hunters and the pride alike—while he talks to his father. At least that's the plan we've decided upon. We have to deal with the matter of Miram first. My vengeance will have to wait until the danger is over.

We left the vehicles at the base of the mountain. Will holds himself tensely, watchful. 'Tamra,' I say for her ears alone as we walk side by side. 'I'm still leaving the pride.'

I'm not sure why I feel compelled to tell her this. As though she, like Will, might doubt my ability to cut ties with the pride. As with him, I hope to correct her of that misapprehension.

'You think so?' A smile plays on her mouth. 'I remember you saying that before.'

'We'll fix things with Miram, settle the score for Dad, and then I'm gone. We'll start over and find Mum just like we—'

'I'm not going.'

I stop to stare at her. Only she keeps walking, so I have to hurry to catch up, sending cautious glances over my shoulder at the others following us. Almost as though I were afraid they've heard her make this announcement.

'What about our plans? What about Mum?'

'Plans change, Jacinda. Besides, I never had much time to think it through. It was your plan. Not mine. I was just so angry over you and Cassian bonding that I wasn't seeing things clearly.'

'That's right. You were mad,' I remind her, 'over my forced bonding. Over the pride banishing Mum. Why do you want to stay here?'

'Because they need me. Not everyone is Severin. I don't want to quit on the entire pride just because of him. He can be removed. He *will* be. Cassian or someone else can take over. It's time for new leadership, and I want to be here to help for that. I need to be. I can be useful and do some good.'

She'd do great things. She's wise and level-headed . . . sees things from all angles. And they'll take her back with open arms. No questions. My breath falls shallow. Leaving the pride for good might translate into a greater loss than I ever imagined if it means losing my sister. There was solace in knowing she was coming with me. But I'll have Will.

'So you'll do this for the pride?' I ask.

'Is that so hard to believe?'

'Um, actually. Yes.' For years she hated the pride— wanted to be free of it forever. I was the one that wanted to stay.

Then she gives herself away.

Her gaze slides ever so slightly away, off to the side.

I follow her eyes to the enormous grey draki, flanking our group. When I look back at her she's facing forward again, trying to pretend I didn't catch her unconscious glance. But it's too late. I saw. I already suspected there was something between the two of them. The beginning of something anyway.

'We all change,' she says vaguely.

'Yes. We do.' I guess Tamra looking at someone else besides Cassian attests to that. She's right. Everything changes . . . evolves. And I feel a sense of anticipation bubble through me, eager for the future to come with Will. Whatever happens, I know we'll be together.

I drop back a few paces, falling into step beside Will. He glances down at me and I smile up at him, just so glad, so relieved to have him here with me.

With my smile I try to convey to him that this isn't forever, that we'll leave soon. I'm not Tamra. The pride might need her, but not me. I'm not going to let Will down—or myself.

He gazes down at me rather intently, curiously.

'This is the place,' Cassian announces as we step into a small break in the forest. He removes his backpack and squares off before a wall of tangled brush. I watch as he begins removing it piece by thorny piece, tossing the branches to the ground and revealing a deep cave.

I step forward and peer inside, surprised to find a stash of supplies already there. I look at Cassian questioningly.

He shrugs. 'You never know. Better safe than sorry.'

'What is this place? Does the pride know about this? Your father?'

'No. Just me.'

I glance again at the bags of food and various gear and equipment, seeing it for what it is—a stockpile. I can't believe Cassian ever thought to take such measures. If the pride was ever in trouble or danger, I just assumed Cassian would go down with it rather than escape. That's what he led me to believe.

Looking over the supplies, I see there are even gemstones. It's not just an emergency stockpile. It's everything a draki would want if he was running away and starting over someplace else. Someplace new.

He finishes clearing the opening and begins checking his supplies, casting me quick glances as he works, clearly sensing my puzzlement.

'You thought about leaving the pride?' I struggle with this—trying to reconcile the Cassian I thought I knew with the Cassian before me.

He's always been about the pride—doing what's best for the community. But this . . . my gaze sweeps the well-stocked cache of supplies. It makes me wonder if maybe Cassian didn't have other plans once. Plans that didn't include becoming the pride's future alpha.

Cassian shrugs yet again and this tips me over from confusion to irritation. He's the one who's been my conscience, the voice in my head that's made me feel so guilty for letting the pride down these past few months. He's the one who's reminded me over and over that the pride is more important than any single one of us. And here he is . . . with an exit plan in place. I let him feel my annoyance at his hypocrisy—for once enjoying that he can sense my emotions.

He blinks and looks away, a flush burning beneath his swarthy skin.

We move into the shelter of the cave. Deghan has to duck his head so it doesn't collide with the low ceiling. Folding his great leathery wings close to his body, he sticks tight to Tamra, joining her as she starts looking through Cassian's stash.

'You should all be fine here until I return.'

Miram inches closer to her brother. 'I don't want you to go. Don't leave me.'

Cassian gives her arm a squeeze. 'You'll be all right. Don't leave the group. They can protect you if you're tracked.'

She whimpers a little and shakes. 'I'm scared, Cassian.'

He hugs her then and my earlier annoyance fades. I understand her fear, her need to cling to Cassian. When I was friendless in the pride, a virtual pariah, I'd clung to him, too. I move close and touch Miram's arm, trying to lend additional comfort.

'I can't take you into the pride. You know that. I promise I won't be gone long. We'll figure this out and you'll be back in your bed before you know it.' He looks at me then as he adds, 'You can trust Jacinda.'

She considers me for a moment and then nods. Strangely enough, I suspect my bonding with her brother reassures her in some way whereas once it bothered her.

Cassian has to peel her arms from around him. He looks from her to me, to each of us. 'I won't be long,' he repeats and then ducks outside. Branches rustle as he arranges them back over the cave's entrance, dousing us in shadowy murk.

Will crouches over the supplies and soon a low glow suffuses the cave from an electric lantern. He rises. The lamp casts him in an eerie yellow light. 'Someone should stand guard outside. I'll go.'

'Are you sure that's a good idea?' All I can think about is one of the pride finding him. Corbin finding him. I shudder, thinking about Cassian's cousin trying to finish what he failed to do before—murdering Will. As dangerous as it is for me, it's more so for him. My stomach dips.

'I'll be careful and stay out of sight,' he assures me, but I'm not placated. He sighs at my grim stare. 'Look, someone has to stand watch. We can't let ourselves get cornered inside this cave.'

Aware of the threat he faces here, I shake my head, frightened to let him go out alone.

'He's right, Jacinda,' Tamra says. She looks at Will. 'We'll take turns.'

Deghan nods, apparently agreeing as well. Still, I can't shake my fear. Am I the only who sees Will wandering alone out there in draki territory as a bad idea?

'I'll go with you.'

'You stay here. You need your rest. You're no good without your strength.' He glances at Miram. 'If hunters show up for her, you'll need to defend her.'

I fold my arms across my chest. My gaze drifts to Miram. She stares at the lantern, looking so young, so vulnerable. So alone without her brother. I chafe my hands up and down my suddenly chilled arms and inch toward her. 'OK. I'll stay.'

Like Cassian, Will leaves, pushing his way through the brush shielding the cave. He carefully repositions the branches after him.

Tamra lowers herself into a sitting position beside Deghan. After a moment, I sit beside Miram, hoping my proximity gives her some comfort. As we settle in, I wonder how Cassian is going to explain everything to the pride—the enkros, me, Will, Deghan. And Miram. I grow antsy thinking how close I am to the pride . . . and to the traitor responsible for my father's death. Even knowing that I have to be patient and wait for things to get settled with Miram doesn't appease me.

Sitting and waiting, I wonder what's to come and whether I'll be ready. Whether any of us will.

CHAPTER EIGHTEEN

I'm laughing and running, ocean water spraying against my calves. I look behind me. Mum and Dad walk hand in hand at a slower pace, just content with this rare vacation away from the pride. Tamra is closing in, fast on my heels, but I'm faster.

Rock formations dot the beach and tower over me. They're beautiful, curious things. Tamra catches up and we laugh, falling against each other and pointing at various outcroppings, commenting on the silly things they remind us of.

'That one looks like a clown.'

'There's a giant rabbit—and that looks like Dad's nose!'

'That one looks like the Eiffel Tower.'

'And that one looks like a palm tree,' Dad says, pointing over my shoulder at the rock formation that is really wide at the top and then tapers down to a thin trunklike shape.

'Hey,' Mum says, fumbling for her camera. 'You two go stand under it.'

I stand beneath it, looking up at the stretch of stone over my head. It sends a faint whisper through my soul, a lot like the earth back home. The rough reddish brown outcropping

fascinates me, and Mum has to shout my name for me to look
at the camera. I turn and smile, tilting my head so that it rests
against my sister.

Then Dad's there, draping an arm around me. He points to
the umbrella of rock above us. 'A palm tree, Jacinda.' He says
this again, smiling.

I nod, smiling back. 'Pretty cool.'

Everything else fades away then. Mum. Tamra. The sound
of the surf. It's just Dad, his eyes gleaming down at me. 'No, it's
a palm tree, Jacinda . . .'

I wake with a gasp, my chest heaving, like I've been running a race. The dimness of my surroundings confuses
me. I don't know where I am. The air is murky, tinged
faintly with a sickly yellow. Strange shadows dance along
dark, uneven walls.

Then it all rushes back over me.

I push myself up and identify Miram curled on her
side on top of her sleeping bag beside me. We must have
fallen asleep talking. I wanted to cheer her up, take her
mind off everything.

As my vision adjusts to the gloom of the cave, a stab
of disappointment fills me. I still see Dad so very clearly,
the image of him crisp and fresh. Almost as if I weren't
dreaming an event from my past at all, but living it again.

Suddenly the back of my throat aches. I can almost
smell the cold sea wind. Dad's voice whispers inside my
ears. *Palm tree.*

My heart jumps in my chest and my pulse begins a fu-
rious hammering against my neck. I don't need to see the
slip of paper my mother left me to remember the words
scrawled upon it.

Remember the palm tree.

At the time, the words hadn't made any sense to me. I trusted that it would come to me, that I would figure it out eventually. And now I have.

I hop to my feet, anxious to give Tamra the news. *I know where Mum is. We can go find her!* Then I stop, my breath expelling in a rush as I remember I can't go anywhere. Not yet. I'm here to get justice for Dad. To help Miram. For Cassian . . . the pride. I have a lot to fix before I'm free to find Mum. I made that decision. This is the reality I've chosen—and dragged Will into with me.

Tamra's chosen something different. I know that's her right . . . but maybe if we have a firm destination, Mum's actual location, she'll come with me.

I resume walking, eager to tell Tamra.

She's nowhere around though. Neither is Deghan. My stomach sinks. It's not hard to guess that they went off somewhere together.

'Tamra?' I call, wondering how long I slept, how long she's been gone.

I walk deeper into the cave, where the lamplight is at its weakest, barely stretching its glow across the cave floor. Suddenly the cave splits, opens to a larger room on the left and a darker, narrower space to my right. I peer into the smaller tunnel. The air feels cooler in that direction.

I glance at the larger space, into the yawning shadows there. Something moves in all the gloom. Like the ripple of a fish against dark waters. I squint and step closer, making out a shape there. I part my lips, ready to call out—

A hand clamps down on my shoulder. 'Jacinda?'

I yelp and spin around. A burst of fire erupts from my lips before I see who's there and manage to retract the heat back inside. Will stands behind me, flinging his hands back in the air like I'm pointing a weapon at him.

'Sorry,' I gasp.

'Hey. Didn't mean to frighten you. Just came to switch with one of you.'

The lamplight haloes him, the yellow glow gilding his brown hair.

The chill from the second cave reaches me, its cool air wrapping me in its embrace, cooling my body's sudden flare of heat. I rub my arms. 'Sorry,' I repeat. 'I'm just jumpy. I can't find Tamra or Deghan.' I motion behind me. 'And I thought I saw something in there.'

Will's gaze fixes beyond my shoulder. A strange look comes over his face. His brow scrunches. He takes a step forward that brings us side by side.

'What the . . .' His voice fades as I spin back around, afraid a hunter lurks there—ready to pounce—that they've found us and somehow crept into the cave.

It's no hunter.

A couple steps into the very edge of light.

'Tamra?' I breathe, the question clear in my voice as I stare at the boy next to her. Boy? He's around our age. Maybe older. But so huge his head nearly scrapes the ceiling of the cave. He's wearing a pair of jeans I recognize as belonging to Cassian, but they fit him snugly around his hips and fall a little short. Further testament to how large he really is.

My gaze sweeps all of him. All *human* him. Starting with the ash blond hair that brushes his shoulders, down to his bare feet. His eyes still possess that wildness, the pupils still vertical slits that give away his savage nature.

I try to speak, try to voice my bewilderment. 'How?'

Tamra smiles. It's a smile I've never seen on her before. It's secretive and vague, but brimming with happiness. 'Deghan's been working on it.'

Deghan nods. 'And Tamra helped me through it. Still feels a little unnatural,' he says, and that's when I notice his accent. He sounds . . . Irish? Where exactly did he and his pride come from? One side of his mouth tips in a smile of sorts. 'Hope I can keep control of myself.'

'You can do it.' Tamra nods, full of brightness and optimism. Not since Chaparral have I seen her like this. Bubbling with hope that her world is suddenly right.

And he brought about this change in her? I don't know whether to hug him or punch him. Fear that Tamra will end up hurt or disappointed again gnaws at me. She's been through enough of that already. Years of that. But the idea that she could find happiness with him . . . it would be better than great.

They're standing so close to each other, and then I notice that they are holding hands, their fingers intimately laced. And it occurs to me that what I think doesn't matter at all. Tamra is already attached to him. I can't influence what they will or won't be. I can merely hope for the best.

Deghan nods at Will. 'Guess I'll take a turn now. Let you get some rest.'

'I'll come with you,' Tamra quickly volunteers. At my arch look, she adds, 'I know the area.'

I watch them walk away, still holding each other's hands. 'Hey,' Will says once we're alone, but what he's really saying—what he's really asking—is whether I'm OK.

169

I drag a hand down the side of my face. 'I guess I suspected this was coming, but still . . .'

'They might be good for each other.'

'How's that?' I ask.

He lifts one shadowy shoulder in a shrug. 'She's new to being a draki . . . and in a way he's new to being human. Maybe they can support each other.'

I angle my head. 'I never thought about it that way.'

'Common ground, you could say.'

I grin at him. 'You're such a smart guy, Will Rutledge.'

'I've been told that before.'

The smile slides from my lips because the sudden thought hits me. *Too smart for me. For this. Too smart to be here getting involved in the mess that is my world.*

'Why on earth are you here with me?' The words fly out before I can stop them. Honestly, the last thing I want is to drive him away.

'That's not obvious?'

I shake my head. I have to be fair to him. That's love, isn't it? Doing what's right, what's best even when it hurts? I can't be selfish and keep him with me when it's just stupid-dangerous for him to be here. And I see that now. I didn't before, but now my fear for him . . . the risks he's taking being here consume me.

I inhale, fill my lungs, and then release the words on a heavy breath. 'If you were smart, you'd walk away from me and never look back.'

He snorts. 'And go back to my dad? That would sort of throw out your theory that I'm smart.'

'There's your grandmother.' He's told me all about his mum's mother in Big Sur. The fact she never got along with Will's dad pretty much is all I need to know to like

170

her. 'She would take you.' Love him. Support him in whatever he wanted to do. Unlike his father.

He nods slowly. 'Are you trying to get me to leave you? Do you *want* me to go? Is that it? Because you can just say so. You don't have to play games with me, Jacinda.'

'I'm not playing with you. I would never—it's . . . complicated.'

'And hasn't it been from the beginning?'

I wince. He's right about that. 'It's just that none of this is fair to you. I'm not fair to you. I've got all this'—I wave my arms—'awful stuff going on and I keep expecting you to suffer through it.'

He's quiet for a moment. I desperately wish I could see his face in the gloom. 'So this is your conscience talking? Making sure I understand the risk I'm taking being here? Believe me, I get it. It's not something I can forget. Just like I won't ever forget the risk you took for me. Remember that?' His eyes gleam through the murk. 'Remember plunging off that cliff after me? Remember manifesting in front of someone you knew to be an enemy? I'll never forget it. It was brave and stupid and selfless. So if I want to be brave and stupid and selfless for you, then just let me.'

We stand toe to toe. Water drips from somewhere in the dark cave. A distant, rhythmic sound that heightens the sudden silence.

I'm not sure who moves first. Me or Will. I just know we're in each other's arms. His hands are in my hair, at my waist, pressing me against him, holding me so tightly I can hardly even draw breath. A good thing because my limbs feel limp, no firmer than jelly. I'm sure if he released me I'd slide to the cave floor in a melted puddle.

Still clinging to each other, he backs me deeper into the cave. It's a little colder, the air clammier now.

And then I can't think any more. Only feel. Savour the drag of Will's mouth down my neck. His hands against my skin. His fingers brush the erratic pulse at my throat and I purr, arch against the warm wall of his chest, pulling him even closer.

His mouth returns to mine, the kiss harder, hungry. The sensitive skin of my lips warms and tingles. My entire body heats, the familiar scald igniting at my core despite the cold cave wall.

Will moans, deepening the kiss. One of his hands slips around my head, angling my face closer. His other hand slides down the length of my neck. His thumb grazes my hammering pulse again and I shudder, placing a palm on the plane of his face, relishing the scrape of his bristly jaw under my fingertips. I savour it all. The press of him over me, the hot fusion of our mouths, the way his hands move on me, always touching, caressing me like I'm something special.

A sharp crack splits the air, like metal on bone.

Suddenly Will's lips are gone, wrenched from mine. All of him vanishes from me, leaving me alone and shivering, arms empty, aching, hands stretching for him in the dark.

I hear him fall with a thud. Bewildered, I crouch, patting the ground, searching for him in the cloying dark. 'Will!'

I brush something. I touch his back, the cotton of his T-shirt cool beneath my fingers. 'Will!' I lightly shake him, roaming my other hand over his body, feeling for an injury. 'Are you hurt? What happened?'

Nothing. He doesn't move. Doesn't utter a sound.

I freeze, suddenly aware I'm not alone. My flesh heats in warning. Another's breath rasps over the air. So close I almost imagine it lifts the strands of hair near my cheek.

My skin contracts and jumps when the voice comes to me out of the dark.

I swing in its direction. The light from the end of the tunnel limns his body. 'Hello, Jacinda.'

CHAPTER NINETEEN

I feel the breadth of him all around me. A draki, in full manifest, his vast wings stretched out defiantly from his body, like he might take flight right here in this cave where the sky is a dead, non-existent thing.

I rise on unsteady legs and start to stagger away but then realize that leaves Will lying defenceless between us. I stop—step over Will, bringing me closer than I want to be to him—but I have no choice. The name shudders past my lips. 'Corbin?'

'Miss me?'

I look down, into the swirling dark below me, where I know Will lies. 'What have you done to him?'

'Just hit him with a rock. Hard.'

'You could have killed him!' I drop down to my knees again. My fingers gently move to his head, locating the bloody gash there.

Everything inside me crumbles and caves in at the possibility that Will could be more than hurt. My voice shakes out, 'We need to get him to a hospital.'

At that suggestion, Corbin laughs mirthlessly. 'You think I give a damn about his life? He's not just a human but a hunter. A hunter who tried to kill me. Who took you.'

I stare up at his shadow. 'What do you want?'

'Cassian is busy right now talking to Severin and the elders, pleading your case.' I don't need light to know that his lip curls with a sneer. I can hear the scorn in his voice. 'He refuses to give up your location until they promise him they won't hurt any of you.' Corbin laughs then, a low, dark sound that curls menacingly around me. 'I don't need Cassian to tell me where he hid you. I haven't been a part of the pride this long, watching my cousin's every move, without knowing about this place. His little sanctuary. Now where's Miram? And Tamra? I'm taking all three of you back.'

'I don't know where they are,' I lie, knowing he won't listen to why Miram can't be brought into the pride yet. He clearly wasn't paying attention when Cassian explained the situation, so why would he believe me?

'What do you mean you don't—?'

'Miram ran away. Tamra went after her.'

He reaches for my arm and hauls me to my feet. 'You're lying. Why are you still hanging around here then? Why didn't you go with Tamra?'

'Someone needed to wait for Cassian.'

'Why did Miram run?' His words punch the air, testing my story.

Steam swells from my nose. 'She was mad that Cassian left her. She's gone . . . probably headed back to the pride.' Desperate hope burns through me that he doesn't bother to check out my story for himself or that if he does

Miram has the sense to use her talent and blend into the walls of the cave. Silence stretches and I know he's thinking, weighing my words.

Hot ash gathers in the back of my throat, and I know I need to force his thoughts away from Miram. 'But I'm not going anywhere with you.' I wrench my arm free.

He grabs me again. 'I thought you might be difficult. That's why I brought this.'

Something glints in the dim light.

'What is—' I bite back the question as I catch the flash of a blade.

Corbin squats and yanks Will up by the back of his hair, the blade poised at his throat. Of course it would mean nothing to him to end Will's life.

'Go ahead,' he taunts, his eyes glinting through the dark. 'Burn me, Jacinda. But I'll be sure to cut his throat first.'

'Corbin,' I whisper hoarsely, 'this isn't you.' But even as I say it, I realize that's just a wish, a hope. Even I know that Corbin is ruthless enough to kill someone he sees as an enemy of the pride, someone keeping him from getting what he wants.

'Fine.' I rise, stepping back. 'Don't hurt him and I'll go with you.' Maybe Tamra and Deghan will find Will and take care of him. It's all I can hope . . . the only thing I can do right now.

'Good to see you using your head. Now, walk in front of me. That way.' He motions to the narrow tunnel. There must be a back way out of this cave, which explains how he snuck up on us. It also explains the cool air I felt earlier.

I march in front of him, my eyes adjusting to the relentless dark. My hand skims the cold, moist wall as I move along, Corbin close behind, prodding my back with the tip of his blade if my steps fall too slowly.

He gives me a particularly sharp jab in the spine and warm blood soaks my shirt, slithers to the small of my back. I glare over my shoulder at the vague shape of him.

'You know you won't always have that knife.'

'I think I can handle you without it, Jacinda.'

I make a sound, part growl, part snort of doubt.

'The problem is you're too soft. You care too much about others. That will always be your downfall . . . and how I can get to you.'

I walk ahead blindly, tears blurring my eyes. I can't even absorb what he's saying to me. I can only think of Will lying back there in the cave, helpless and bleeding.

'Speed it up. I can't wait to show up with you. Maybe then they'll stop listening to Cassian and pay me some respect.'

'He's your cousin,' I accuse. 'Why do you act like he's your enemy?'

'Because while he may be next in line, I'm the one who deserves it. What has Cassian done besides being born Severin's son? Nothing. I'd be a better alpha than him. He cares too much. Like you. It affects his judgment. I'd do what's right for the pride, no emotions, no questions asked.'

'I bet you would,' I grumble.

Light emerges ahead, growing brighter and bigger as we advance. I duck my head and step out into a heavy thicket. Trees and brush scratch us at every side. We claw our way through, squeezing along the narrow path that Corbin took to get into the cave.

Blinking so my eyes adjust, I see that the light isn't as bright as I first thought. Dusk has fallen. Tiny motes of dust dance on the dull beams of yellow. He nudges me to keep going.

'What do you think is going to happen, Corbin? You're just going to show up with me and they'll—'

'They'll see that *I* get things done. When something needs to happen I make it happen. After I deliver you, I'll find Miram and Tamra, too.'

I glance over my shoulder. The fading light hits his face and his fervour is captured there, bright and intense in his purply black eyes. His eyes are nothing like Cassian's though.

There's something dead there, unfeeling. Something desperate and ugly.

'You don't understand what's happening.' I motion back toward the cave. 'If you would just listen to Cassian—'

'I have no desire to listen to Cassian.'

'It's about Miram. Something happened to her—'

'Spare me. You don't expect me to believe you actually care about Miram.'

'I expect *you* to care about her—and the safety of the pride. If you really think you are leadership material and want what's best for the pride you'd hear me out.'

'Enough!' He forces me around and shoves his face close to mine. The knife pricks me in the ribs.

I glance down, then back up at him, feeling coldly calm inside. 'You've totally lost it,' I whisper.

'I've had enough of never being heard. Of no one listening. No one caring. Especially you. You've walked around the pride for years looking down your nose at me.' He smiles slowly. 'Well, I have your attention now, don't I?'

'Your knife does,' I reply, unable to keep the defiant edge from my voice—even with a weapon pointing at me.

'Same thing. Now, turn around.'

'You think your uncle will approve if you hurt me?'

'You do what I say, and it won't come to that. Besides, my uncle has had his fill of you.' He angles his head. The thin, vertical pupils of his eyes quiver. 'If I got rid of you he might just thank me.'

A metallic sour taste coats my mouth. I remind myself this could very well be true. After all, Severin was already corrupt enough to kill one of our own. Maybe he would turn a blind eye if Corbin harmed me.

I allow Corbin to nudge me into motion again. I soon recognize the area. The pulsing trees, the whispering wind. Only a few miles and we'll reach the pride. I can't let him bring me in like some kind of prisoner. I've had enough of that role to last a lifetime. And my appearance might disrupt any ground Cassian has made with Severin. I can't risk that.

And there's Will. I have to get back to him. I close my eyes in a pained blink, thinking about him lying hurt and alone. What will happen to him if Corbin informs everyone he left a hunter unconscious on the cave floor? I can't let them find him like that—defenceless. Easy prey.

Cassian. I whisper his name inside myself. Let it float through me like a familiar breeze. *Corbin has me. We're coming.* I know he can't read my thoughts, but hopefully he'll understand enough from my emotions. I wait, probing inside me, trying to find Cassian there. He must be too preoccupied dealing with his father. I get nothing but a faint hum of him. Just enough to let me know he's there and OK.

I scan the familiar trees, my ears perking, listening for anything out of the ordinary in the vanishing light. Something to latch on to as a distraction.

Nothing. Grimly, I accept that I'm going to have to invent my own instead.

Satisfied with the thickness of the trees to my right, I stop. 'What's that?'

'Keep walking.'

I ignore his hard shove. 'No. Listen.'

'I don't hear anything.'

I turn to face him. 'Shut up then and listen unless you relish the idea of hunters finding us.'

His eyes narrow on me suspiciously, but he cocks his head and listens.

I watch him, barely breathing, waiting for the right moment . . .

And then he does it. Glances away for a split second to peer into the foliage for potential hunters.

It's all I need. I dive for the nearby trees. Corbin shouts behind me, but I don't stop. My muscles bunch and burn as I tear through the trees. As I move, I struggle free of my shirt. My wings unfurl from my body, snapping on the air.

I push hard, working my legs and pumping my arms— resisting that instinctive urge to fly. He'd see me at once if I took off above the trees. Still, I use my wings for momentum, flapping them to increase my speed. I know Corbin's doing the same. I glance up several times to make sure he's not flying overhead and about to land on top of me. No sight of him in the sky and I push on.

He's terribly loud, a beast of nightmare crashing through the undergrowth, almost blocking out the sound of running water from the nearby river.

He shouts my name and I shiver, thinking about that knife in his hand. If he catches me again, I'm not sure he won't use it on me.

I may not have any choice but to resort to my best defence—my fire. This makes me tremble harder—the idea of killing one of my own, a fellow draki, Cassian's cousin. Even if he is trying to hurt me, I don't want that. I don't want *this*.

He's still coming strong, roaring my name. Our Evasive Manoeuvres teacher would definitely give him poor marks for the racket he's making. If any hunters are nearby on Miram's trail he's making it easy for them to track us.

I weave through the trees, jumping over rotting logs and vine-thick bushes. I launch into the air and touch down on a boulder embedded deeply into a rise. I don't go far. Just inch back and hide myself behind a drape of limbs and leaves.

High up in my perch, I hold my breath and wait. Corbin whips past, half flying, half running, his curses burning my ears. I wait, listen as he fades into the forest.

Then I burst from my hiding spot and fly back the way we came, to the cave, urgency giving me fresh energy. Once I get there, I tear free the foliage obscuring the front of the cave and burst inside, gasping, knowing I don't have much time. When Corbin can't find me he'll know that I circled back here.

Miram lifts her head from where she rests on a pallet, levelling her blank gaze on me. For a moment, I glance around, expecting to see my sister, but then I remember she and Deghan took a turn guarding the outside of the cave.

At that moment they rush inside behind me, breathless, apparently too distracted with each other to be very good guards. Good thing I wasn't a hunter.

'Jacinda? Where—how—'

'Corbin found us. There's a back way into this cave.' I run deeper, into the dark, to Will, calling over my shoulder, 'Watch out! He's still out there!'

Tamra says something behind me, but her voice is an echo as I dive into the narrow tunnel at the rear of the cave, searching for Will. I find him where we left him. Crouching, I touch him, so relieved I almost sob when I feel the rise of his chest. He's still breathing. Still alive.

'Here.' Deghan's voice sounds from the dark beside me. 'I got him.' Without a sound, he lifts Will and carries him into the front of the cave. Once in the light, I inspect the damage. The gash doesn't look as deep as I feared. The bleeding had stopped.

'Will,' I say, squeezing his shoulder.

He moans and swats my hand away from him.

'I think he's going to be OK,' Deghan announces. 'He's coming around. And it doesn't look too dangerous a wound.'

Will blinks slowly, squinting against the moderate light as though it stings his eyes. He focuses on my face. 'Jacinda? What happened?'

I shake my head. Even if he could understand me, there's no time for long explanations. Grasping Will's arm, I help him to his feet. Will winces. We need to get out of here before Corbin shows up again. Him or others.

There's a good chance he went back and told the pride where they could find me. *Us.*

'Jacinda?' I turn at the sharpness of Tamra's voice. She's not looking at me though. I follow her gaze.

She's looking at Miram's pallet. The *empty* pallet. The wadded-up jacket Miram used as a pillow is still there— but she's not. She's not anywhere.

'Miram,' Tamra calls, looking around us, turning her whole body as if she'd find the girl lurking somewhere, in some small dark corner of the cave. True, Miram is a visiocrypter, who can make herself invisible, but I somehow doubt that's what happened. Not seeing her, Tamra stops and faces me and announces what I already know: 'She's gone.'

CHAPTER TWENTY

I demanifest and pull my shirt back over my head. We leave the cave in quick order. Will is walking but slow moving, and I insist on helping him, draping his arm over my shoulder as we move through the trees.

'She went this way.' Deghan leads us, studying the ground and the fresh shoeprints there.

'To the river,' Tamra mutters with a shake of her head. 'What's she thinking, leaving the group? She knows she's the one most in danger.'

'She hasn't been right since she learned about the homing device,' I say.

Will labours for breath as he tries to keep up with our pace. The forest is quiet, the sound of burbling water draping over the stillness. The last rays of sunlight filter down through the trees, striking Tamra's hair and giving it a silver cast.

I know these mountains, this forest, and I can't recall it ever being this quiet. Something isn't right. Naturally my mind drifts to the hunters. I recall every time they chased me. They were never quiet. Their vehicles and choppers always announced their presence. Sometimes too late, but I always heard them before I saw them.

For some reason, I don't think it will be like that again. If they have the device that's going to lead them directly to Miram, then they'll use stealth and surprise to attack her.

The sound of rushing water grows closer. For the first time, these trees don't feel like the solace they've always been to me. In every blade of grass, in every whispering limb, behind every tree trunk lurks a potential menace.

I look around sharply and dig my fingers into Will's hand. Solid, bigger than mine, it gives me strength. He looks down at me and I start to tell him my misgivings . . . the bad feeling in my gut, but Deghan holds up a hand, stopping us at the tree line edging the riverbank.

I step out from beneath the weight of Will's arm. I must look as worried as I feel because he nods once at me as he leans back against a tree. 'Go on,' he says quietly. 'I'll be fine.'

Fresh blood dribbles from the gash on his forehead. This close to him, the coppery aroma fills my nose and I'm suddenly more concerned about him than hunters. His eyes look dazed, his expression tight, like he's focusing on being OK, willing it to be so, but it's just not the case.

'Will,' I whisper, gently shaking his shoulder. 'Are you all right?'

He blinks slowly and nods, his gaze fastening on me and coming into focus, looking less glassy. 'I'm fine.'

Believing him, the air expels from my hotly contracting lungs. I smooth my palm over his cheek, already scratchy and in need of a shave. Just the sensation of him against my hand, whole and alive and with me, the hum of his lifeblood murmuring beneath his flesh, buoys me.

Deghan holds back a branch and motions for me to check out whatever he and Tamra are looking at. I hesitate, staring uncertainly at Will, hating to leave him.

'Go,' he urges.

Nodding once, I move ahead to see why we've stopped. Crouching beside Deghan, I follow his gaze and see his caution is needless.

There are no hunters, despite the warning prickle at the back of my neck. Miram stands across the river from us with her aunt Jabel. Miram clings to her, her lips moving.

'It's just her aunt,' I whisper, still glancing around, an eye for the shadows nestled between the trees where I worry that hunters hide, watching, waiting for the moment to pounce.

I sink down, my heels digging into the yielding earth, intent on staying hidden. Safety always lies in that, it seems—staying hidden.

Jabel nods sympathetically as Miram talks, doubtlessly explaining her predicament. Several moments pass before Jabel folds her niece into her arms, smoothing a hand over her loose hair. Emotion tugs at my heart. Jabel is her aunt, sure, but she's never been the warm, welcoming type. It's nice to see the evidence of her love for her niece.

What epitomizes Jabel is her sharp, watchful gaze. So like her son, Corbin. Her very nature as a hypnos draki always made me uneasy. Hard to imagine she and Mum had once been the best of friends. I'm humbled at this softer, kinder image, glad for the comfort Miram finds in her.

Then it happens.

I don't have time to move, much less make a sound. There's no chance to shout out a warning, no chance to understand . . . to process until it's too late.

We can only watch, gawking as Jabel lifts a blade from inside her sleeve and plunges it into Miram's back.

Tamra chokes on a cry beside me as Jabel twists the blade, pulling it back and stabbing it in a second time before shoving Miram into the river. Eyes burning, I stare wide-eyed. My mouth parts, opens on a silent scream. My heart crashes against my chest, a painfully beating hammer inside me.

Behind me something snaps. I swing around to find Corbin standing there, his expression horrified as he looks over our heads to his mother. To his cousin.

Clearly, he knew nothing of his mother's plans, nor suspected her of being capable of this.

In that moment, staring at his paled features, he's the boy I grew up with. And he just witnessed his mother murder his cousin. I reach for his hand. He yanks it away, shaking his head fiercely like he can't believe his eyes. 'No,' he croaks. 'No!'

Spinning around, he tears through the brush, fleeing what he can't face. Blinking, I stare after him, astonished. I suppose I half expected him to confront Jabel. She's his mother, after all. He can't be afraid of her, can he?

I turn back and watch as the undulating current carries Miram's body away like she's weightless. I can't move, can only stare in shock as she rushes past us on top of the water. Her eyes are vacant, staring up at the sky sightlessly.

187

I quickly duck to the side and heave, retching into a nearby bush. My body shakes and shudders, numb fingers grasping the thorny, silvery green leaves. Will steps past and peers out at the river to see for himself what has me puking up my guts.

I lift my head and rejoin them all, my unsteady limbs quivering as we watch Miram's killer matter-of-factly lower herself to her knees at the bank of the river, and clean her knife off in the water. Calm and serene, Jabel's face reveals nothing, no emotion, no regret for the murder she just committed. And I know, feel the truth in my bones . . . I'm staring at the same person who betrayed my father. It wasn't Severin, but his sister.

'What do we do?' Tamra whispers.

I can't recall a draki ever killing another in cold blood. This is even different from tricking my father into getting captured. Bereft of any human decency. Miram was her niece. Maybe it happened long ago, back in the days of the Great Wars, when we were primitive, warring tribes—maybe then we cut one another down on a whim. But not now. Not any more. We're more enlightened. That's what I've always been taught. Humans are the killers, the ones who commit crimes against their own kind. Not us.

'She can't get away with it,' I announce grimly. I turn and face Will. 'Can you find your way back to the car?'

'What?' He blinks, his gaze focusing on me.

Maybe it's something in his face, but I have to look away from him right then. I glance at my sister and Deghan. 'The pride has to be told. Right away. Jabel can't get away with this. She's a danger.'

I feel Will's stare and look back at him. He studies me for a moment before turning away, staring at the lush trees as if seeing them for the first time. 'You'll never be finished with any of this,' he murmurs.

I wet my suddenly dry lips, ready to explain how everything just changed and I'm needed here. *Again*. That I'm going to walk directly into the pride and demand a judgment and I can't bring Will with me. I need him out of harm's way while all this goes down. I can't be worried about his safety. 'Will—'

He holds up a hand to stop me. 'I can find my way.' And then he's moving. Walking away from me.

I lunge for him. He twists free, not even slowing down.

I call out, 'I'll meet you—'

He whirls around. His hazel eyes gleam fire. 'I'd have to wait forever. Because you'll never come.'

The words hit me like a slap. He continues through the trees again, leaving me. My chest tightens as his back disappears from view. *From me*.

'Jacinda,' Tamra urges right behind me, 'we can handle this. Go after him.'

I look at Tamra . . . over her shoulder at the small figure of Jabel disappearing through the branches.

'Go, Jacinda,' Tamra insists.

Desperation stirs in my chest. It's time to end this splitting myself between two worlds, this sense of forever being torn in half, pulled in two directions.

My sister is right. She can deal with this. I can let go.

'I'll be back . . . or in touch,' I say finally, looking anxiously to the spot where Will disappeared. If nothing else, Tamra and I have to communicate about Mum. I don't really know if I'll ever be back. I only know that I'm leaving with Will.

Decision made, I take off after Will. Pushing through the foliage, I dart between trees, certain he's not too far ahead. Especially not so recently injured. In fact, I eye the ground ahead, hoping he hasn't passed out from his head injury. I should have never let him go without me.

It's the quiet again that alerts me. I can't hear Will ahead of me no matter how I strain for the sound of him. I stop and listen hard, my nerves stretched tight.

'Will,' I say in a loud whisper, suddenly conscious that I shouldn't yell his name.

I look up, too, not forgetting Corbin. Although hunting me is probably the last thought on his mind now. There's nothing in the sky. I move on, only this time slower, wondering where Will disappeared to. At my pace, I should have caught up with him by now. Shaking my head, I press on, knowing the direction he took and determined to find him.

A bird calls out over the silent wood and I stop, my skin snapping tight. I know this forest, the creatures and sounds that exist here. And that birdcall was far from natural. It doesn't fit into the world pulsing all around me. As savvy a tracker as Will is, he's probably aware of the danger, too.

I spin around, intent on turning back for Tamra and Deghan. They need to be warned that we're not alone. And I'm hopeful Will may have changed his mind and backtracked as well when he realized that there's something else here besides us. Our chances of survival are better together.

I plunge ahead, weaving a path through thick tree trunks, my bare palms reaching out to scrape rough bark as I move. A reminder that I'm alive.

I grasp one tree to swing around it—and smack directly into something hard. Thrown off balance, I reach out with both hands to steady myself and come upon a relentless wall. My fingers flex. Warm male.

I look up at a familiar face. 'Xander,' I mouth, unable to find my voice. My pulse locks before leaping into overdrive, hammering against my skin. I back up a step, but his hands clamp around my wrists.

I look left and right, wildly searching for Will. As if he will miraculously appear to save me from his cousin. Even as I wish it, I know that's not going to happen.

I swallow my fear. Other hunters must be close. Even though he's hunted by himself before, Xander's not out here solo this time. I can feel them. I know they're here . . . just like I know *why* they're here. They're on Miram's trail. Miram who's now dead, floating downstream.

My heart constricts as I think about them finding her. Just a girl. Not the 'dragon' they expect. What will they think? If Jabel killed Miram because of the risk she posed to the pride, she evidently failed to consider hunters finding the corpse of a human girl with a tracking device inside her that had been implanted in a draki.

I take in Xander's appearance. He's outfitted in full camo, a tranq gun slung over his shoulder. He's not holding the locating device, but I know someone else is . . . one of the other hunters in his group.

'Jacinda?' he demands, his voice incredulous, bewildered. 'What are you doing here? Where's Will?' The question of the hour. He squeezes my wrists harder, and I wince. 'Where's my cousin?'

'I—I don't know. I lost him.' That much is true, at least. 'He's around here somewhere.' I hope.

Xander stares at me so intently, his dark eyes probing and suspicious. 'Come with me.'

With one hand circling my wrist, I don't have much choice. Not if I want to look like some hapless human girl who simply got lost in these woods. And that's all I can be. All I can let him see.

He rotates a small black mouthpiece near his lips. 'Hey, we've got a situation here. I'm coming in.'

They haven't fanned out too far from one another. In seconds, we meet up with a dozen other hunters, all out-fitted in similar gear. I recognize Angus and a few others. They stare at me with equal shock.

'What's she doing here?' Angus demands.

'Isn't that the girl Will was hooking up with?' another asks, pointing at me with his tranq gun.

Xander slaps the weapon away with an annoyed grunt. 'Watch where you point that, idiot. Apparently she's still his girlfriend.' Xander regards me scornfully. 'I'm betting she's the reason Will ran off.' He shakes his head as if this idea is beyond ridiculous to him.

To them, I'm nothing. Merely a stupid girl too nosy for her own good. I'm safe as long as they think that. I have to get them off this mountain before they learn the truth.

'What do we do with her?' Angus leans toward Xander, saying in what he imagines to be discreet tones, 'We're here to—'

'I know what we're here to do.' Xander's black-eyed gaze settles on me. 'And I'm figuring she knows why we're here, too.'

I suck a breath deep inside my constricting lungs. He *knows* I know? He can't possibly remember what I am.

That I'm the thing that he hunts. My muscles tighten and brace. If it comes down to it, I'll have to try outrunning them. I can't expose myself as a draki in front of them. There's no Tamra here to shade them.

Xander cocks his head, pinning me with his gaze. And I feel like that—a bug pinned to the spot in some experiment. 'Will told you about us, didn't he?'

I blink, pull back ever so slightly. Realizing admitting this doesn't out me, I nod. 'Uh, yeah.'

Xander grunts, like he knew as much. He looks to the others. 'Just like I thought. He told her! She's got him whipped.'

Angus steps closer to me, his face ruddier than I remember. Sweat carries like steam off his stocky frame. I turn my face away from the intense odour. 'So what are you doing here now?' he demands, no notion of the term personal space.

I think fast. 'I wanted to see for myself. I told Will I wanted to see . . . them.' I almost slipped. Almost called us draki—a term these hunters don't use. To them, we are simply dragons.

They all look mad now. Angry and dangerous. Like, if they could get their hands on Will . . . my mind shies from the thought. He's far safer with them than with my pride.

And yet you brought him here, to this dangerous place, practically in the lap of the pride.

'Wait till his dad hears about this,' Angus says with relish. 'Ain't no forgiving Will then.'

Xander's top lip curls against his teeth. 'He won't care. He wants Will back too much. With his particular skills, his father will let even this slide.'

He means Will's uncanny ability to track my kind. Only they have no idea just how deep that skill runs. I shiver, thinking about his powers. If they found out he'd never be free of them.

'Well, we can't keep her around *and* complete our mission,' one of the older hunters says to the group. He looks to be in his mid-twenties. He hardly spares a glance for me, too preoccupied with the device he holds in his hands—a locator box exactly like the one the other hunters had.

Just like I thought, they were here for Miram. He shakes the black box and moves it in a wide arc around him. 'It's moving fast. That way.' He gestures to the right. 'We gotta go. Now.'

He's pointing in the direction of the river and Miram's body drifting with the current. Away but not fast enough. With the locator, they'll always have a read on her. They'll find her. *And the truth.*

'I know my way back to the car.' I wince inside at how eager and squeaky my voice sounds. 'That's probably where Will went,' I add with a forced shrug and move to leave. 'I'll tell him you're all looking for him—'

Xander grabs my hand. 'I don't think so, Red. You can come with us. He'll turn up.' He looks me up and down with a sort of smirk on his face. 'With you he always does. And when he shows up, we'll put him to work doing what he does best—hunting dragons.' He nods at the device the older hunter holds. 'And then you'll get your wish, sweetheart.'

The last thing I can say is that they're chasing a ghost, so I say nothing as he pulls me along.

CHAPTER TWENTY-ONE

I'm swept forward by the group. The beeping locator takes us closer to the river, so there's no chance
the thing isn't working. I strain to glimpse the red
blinking lights, trying to see how close we are to
Miram. The beeping grows louder as we approach
the rushing water, matching the rhythm of my racing
pulse.

We stop at the bank, water rushing past us.

'I don't see anything,' Angus announces unnecessarily.

Xander takes the locator from the other hunter and
hits it a few times as if that will somehow help the reading. 'This thing says we're right on top of it.'

It. My throat burns ash and char. That's all I am. All
we'll ever be to them. As hunters, how could they see
anything else?

Will does. Did.

I look around me, desperately searching as if I'll suddenly spot him. I hope it's as Xander predicted and he'll
find us. Find me.

Scanning my surroundings, I don't see Will. But something else catches my eye. Downstream to the left, a dam of logs and leaves stretches out halfway across the river. She's hard to detect amid the varying shades of brown, but Miram's body is caught there, tangled in the twist of branches and rotting wood. I hold my breath, hoping the water will manage to pull her free and sweep her downriver before they see her.

'Over there! What's that?'

My heart sinks. I blink once, slow and miserable at the exclamation. The hunters around me erupt into conversation, speculation over what could be caught up in the dam. They move to the edge of the riverbank. One of the hunters walks tentatively across the unstable dam, hands stretched out at his sides for balance.

Let it break. Let it break.

He crouches down and prods at Miram with his weapon. 'It's a girl! She's not moving. Dead.'

Xander waves an arm. 'Bring her in.'

As the hunter drags Miram's body from the dam, I edge back step by slow step while all their attention is centred on Miram. This might be my best chance to escape. To find Tamra so she can shade them into forgetting everything.

Miram's body is dropped limply onto the shore. Her face looks waxy, the shock still etched there in her unseeing eyes. The hunters crowd around her.

'What happened to her?'

'Damned dragons. Bet they did this to her.'

The locator is louder now, the beeps coming faster with Miram this close. Xander frowns intently, a look of concentration settling in the stark lines of his face. I watch as he glances from the locator to Miram, panic rising sharply inside me. It won't be long before he figures it out.

I slide one more step away from them, and then another, prepared to bolt, when I sense someone behind me.

I look over my shoulder, stop a second before bumping into the hulking chest.

'Going somewhere?' Angus leers down at me. I didn't realize he wasn't with the others.

'No,' I deny. 'I just don't want to see a dead body. It's not exactly on my to-do list.'

He snorts. 'Too bad. You're here . . . just like you wanted, right?'

Right. That's what I alluded to . . . that I wanted a taste of Will's secret life.

Angus takes my arm and yanks me towards the group. My feet drag against the rocky riverbank. The group of hunters continues to speculate.

'Poor thing,' one mutters. 'She's so young.'

Xander stands above Miram, looking unmoved as he waves the locator over her, sending it into a frenzy of beeping.

'The locator must be broken,' someone says.

'No, it's not,' Xander proclaims, studying Miram in a way that increases my unease. 'It's working. The homing device has to be inside her.'

'Why is it inside a *girl?* It can't be.'

Angus's grip loosens around my arm as he steps forward to inspect Miram. I slip my arm free and linger a few feet behind him, cautioning myself to wait. If I take off running, they'll notice.

'There's one way to find out.' Xander pulls a blade from his vest and crouches over her.

The hunter most affected by the sight of Miram objects. 'We can't just cut her up! She's a human—'

'Not any more. Now she's a corpse.' Xander moves towards her, his lips a straight, humourless line.

Bile surges inside my throat. And I can't stay. I can't witness them carve up Miram.

'Look at her blood,' a voice suddenly says. 'It's dragon blood.'

Choking back a cry, I turn to flee just as Will emerges from the trees onto the riverbank.

'Will!' I run for him. He catches me up in his arms, squeezing me so tightly he crushes the breath from me. He pulls back to look down at me, framing my face in his hands. 'I'm sorry I left—'

'No, I'm sorry,' I say, shaking my head. 'You were right.'

Our voices are low and feverish, our lips close. His sharp gaze flicks once over my shoulder, taking in everything, everyone, in a glance before settling back on me.

I swallow and mouth the words more than I speak them, 'They found Miram. Her blood . . .'

He nods tightly. 'They'll figure it all out soon.'

I nod in agreement. 'Yes, once they get past the denial and disbelief, they'll know.'

He slides his hand from my face and seizes one of my hands, lacing his fingers tightly with mine.

Just this touch, his strong grip, makes me feel better, emboldened. Not alone. It's the jolt of strength I need.

'Don't worry. We're not going to be here when that happens.' He doesn't even make a full turn before his name is called.

'Will!'

A shudder ripples through me.

Will's grip tightens on me as he faces his cousin, his . . . *family*. His expression reveals nothing, the perfect implacable mask as he nods in acknowledgment at each member of the group.

In a few short strides Xander's before him. 'Your dad's been worried. He thought you went to your grandmother but she said she hasn't seen you, not that we trusted that old hag. Where've you been?'

Will shrugs, the only answer he's going to give apparently.

Xander stares unblinking.

The silence stretches uncomfortably. I look between the two of them, glad at least that attention is off Miram. Off me. But the moment doesn't last.

The oldest hunter of the group looks anxious, annoyed at this distraction. 'C'mon,' he says, waving a knife over Miram. 'Are we going to do this or what?'

Xander suddenly grins. 'Why don't we have Will here do it?'

He wants Will to cut into Miram? My stomach heaves. My fingers press into Will's hand, willing him not to do it . . . to come up with another way out of this.

'We were just leaving,' Will says.

Xander looks from me to Will, his dark gaze sweeping over our clasped hands. 'What's the rush?' He steps between us, clapping Will on the shoulder and dragging him along. 'C'mon. We could really use your help. This is your thing, after all.'

From his arch look, I know he doesn't want or need Will's help. He's simply pushing Will into this because

Will doesn't want to do it. He wants to get under his skin. He thrives on it. Same as always.

Several heavy moments pass. The hunters all stare at Will, sizing him up. Will shoots me a meaningful glance and moves forward. Xander's hawk gaze notes the look. His black eyes narrow on me and I feel the old familiar tightness in my chest—the sense that he sees more in me than he should. And maybe now he does. He was the first to imagine that the tracking device was in Miram, maybe he's already coming to his own conclusions about me.

Every nerve ending in my body burns, sizzles, the draki desperate to come out, to protect myself, protect Will—*survive*. Because everything about being here, right now in this moment with these hunters, screams danger. More than any other time before.

The air thickens into something I can touch. Dense and suffocating. A gust rolls over me, lifting the hair off my shoulder. My skin tightens, stings with awareness. I scan the river, the caps on the water's surface. Lush trees rustle with a sudden wind. I look up. Nothing mars the skyline. Yet.

I have to get Will out of here. Now.

I swallow back the acrid burn in my throat and inch forward to where they stand over Miram. I grasp Will's sleeve and give it a sharp tug.

He doesn't show that he even feels me. I glance longingly over my shoulder to the cover of the trees, looking back as Xander slaps a knife into Will's hand.

'The enkros plant a homing device in the head of every dragon captured,' Xander explains, his dark eyes dead cold.

'How is it we didn't know that?' Will asks.

'I guess we never knew because we never needed to. No dragon ever escaped before.'

'Well, there you go,' Will says with a shrug, motioning to Miram. 'That's a girl. Not a dragon. She can't have one in her.'

The older hunter holds up the black box. 'This locator says she does.'

'It must be wrong. Broken,' Will returns.

'But her blood.' Angus points to the knife wound. 'What's *that* about?'

'Well.' Will motions to his chest and then to the group at large. 'That can be for other reasons, you know.' I watch in awe, impressed at his calm level-headedness in this situation. He smiles, trying to disarm them. It doesn't work.

'Yeah, I don't think she's the wonder freak that you are,' Xander says sharply, bitterly, as he takes the knife from Will. He tosses it lightly, easily catching it by the grip. 'Something's off here, and I think you know more than you're saying.' His gaze slides to me. 'I'm going to figure it out.' With a firm nod, he squats and holds up the blade, prepared to cut into Miram.

I suck in a breath and tear my gaze away, unable to watch but unable to leave Will either. No more leaving each other. Ever.

The wind intensifies then. My hair whips around my face, lashing my cheeks. I scrape the strands free just in time to see a dark blur flash before my eyes, the gust of air knocking me to the ground.

I swipe the wild tangle of hair from my face, watching as Cassian lands on Xander with his clawed hands and feet outstretched and rips him off the ground.

Everyone gawks, frozen.

Xander writhes and dangles like a worm on a hook. Cassian's great leathery wings work, sleek black sails churning the air.

He thinks Xander killed his sister. I know this instantly, feel the full force of his wrath like a knife slicing a path through me, and I know there will be no controlling his fury. His emotion engulfs me, so strong it knocks me off my feet.

As the hunters come alive, shouting and fumbling for their weapons, Cassian flings Xander high. He somersaults several times in the air before he collides with a tree. Branches and bones crack as Xander drops violently down through a labyrinth of branches. Just as quickly as he appeared, Cassian's gone.

Again, everyone falls still.

Will and I stare, a frozen tableau alongside the hunters. No one breathes as Xander remains motionless on the ground in a broken, lifeless heap. I suck in a breath, surprised at the wrench in my chest. I don't feel *nothing* for Xander. He's my enemy, yes, but pity rises up in me nonetheless.

My hands dig and curl into soil as I scan the sky. Leaves whisper like a child's song in the trees, but there's no sight of Cassian anywhere. It's like he's vanished. But I know he's here, a dark spectre lurking, watching us, readying for his next move—the inevitable attack. Even if I didn't know this about him, I can *feel* him. Feel his deadly purpose coursing through me, spreading like venom. Unstoppable.

For a moment, my gaze catches on the glassy eyes of Miram. In that second it seems like she's staring right at me—*through* me. But there's no life there any more. She doesn't see me. With her dead, I know that Cassian won't let a single one of these hunters survive. Not while he believes them to be responsible. He'll die himself before letting even one of them escape. He'll see they pay for his sister's death. Xander is just the first.

Then, I blink. Snap back to myself. 'Will.' My voice sounds loud, discordant and jarring in the stunned silence.

Several hunters start at the sound, glancing at me and swinging their weapons in my direction, thoughtlessly. Or deliberately. Their eyes are wild, every movement a panicked jerk. I swallow down the burning char in my mouth, feel the smoke fill my nose and hope they don't notice this.

As though my voice triggers him, Angus shouts curses up into the air, rotating his stocky frame in a frenzied circle. 'Come out! Come out, scum!'

He starts firing his weapon. Not one of the tranq guns. They've all switched from tranq guns to other firearms—rifles, crossbows. They're no longer here to retrieve. They're here to kill. Just like Cassian.

Fire burns up my windpipe and there's no fighting my fear.

'Will,' I say again, my voice a growling rumble, revealing that I'm half lost already.

Will reaches out and grabs my hand. His fingers hold tight to mine. He nods hard at the trees, and I nod back, understanding.

Together we run for the trees.

'Hey!' Angus yells after us and I hear the pound of running feet, someone, one of them coming after us. A quick glance over my shoulder confirms this. It's another hunter—the older one with his serious face and hard eyes.

A moment after I see him, darkness flashes before my eyes like a great black veil cast down. Cassian. Again, he's there, filling the near darkness.

Gunfire explodes on the air in sharp pops, but it doesn't stop Cassian from sweeping the hunter off his feet and disappearing with him into the trees.

It's chaos everywhere as the hunters shout frenzied instructions at one another. 'He's picking us off!'

'We've got to get out of here!'

'Like hell! Let's go after him!'

We're almost to the trees when suddenly a shuddering wind lifts the hair off my shoulders and whips it all around me. Looking up, I see another draki descending.

'No!' I cry thickly. *Corbin.*

He snatches my arm and pulls me off my feet. My legs flail in the air.

Will shouts and jumps, trying to reach me. But I'm already too high.

The hunters redirect their attention to me and Corbin. Bullets and arrows fly.

I hear Will's panicked cry. 'Look out! You're going to hit her!'

They're not too concerned. An arrow flies so close it grazes my hair with a whistle. It misses me, but not Corbin. The arrow strikes him in the chest, impales deeply into the muscle of his pectoral. He wraps a hand around the arrow's shaft. His purply blood flows thickly between his fingers.

He howls and we tailspin through the trees, my legs flying as if they're made of nothing. He lands hard on his back. I'm sprawled half over him, half on the ground. I push up with the heels of my palms, careful not to prod the arrow.

I look down at this boy I grew up with. Despite what we've become, he's been part of my life as far back as my earliest memory. His face contorts with pain, his ridged nose flaring in and out quickly . . . like he can't draw air in fast enough. I don't wish this even on him.

'Corbin,' I say, but his name comes out more a sob. I cover my mouth and choke back the sound.

He's alive now, and if he can make it back to the pride he might pull through this. My jaw locks tight as resolve steals over me. I can't let them kill him. As crazy and selfish as he's been, I believe he was trying to save me just now. And he got shot for his trouble.

The hunters charge through the trees at us with weapons poised.

Will shouts for them to stop, waving his arms wide as he dives into the fight. 'You're going to hit her!' He tackles one hunter before he can lift his gun in our direction.

Angus breaks ahead of the group, pulling a knife free, and I know he intends to use it on Corbin. Finish him. With a bellow, he lifts it high.

My gaze swings to Corbin, defenceless on the ground. His eyes stare widely, lost in pain. None of the usual hard contempt etches his face. He looks so young and frightened. Like the boy I went to primary school with who stammered out his answers.

My mind works feverishly. He's a big target. I can't shield him. I can only do . . . *it*.

Use that part of myself—the thing that I am.

Sliding my hand off Corbin, I rise to my feet in one easy move and stand directly in front of him, bracing myself for what's to come. For what I'm about to do.

Chapter Twenty-Two

For a minute, it seems like everything stops. Someone hit the pause button on everyone except me.

Angling my head, I look around at all the still figures, the frozen expressions, bodies halted in motion. I stare and absorb it all with an eerie sense of calm.

And then we all begin to move again. But only like underwater creatures, fighting against the fluid all around us, trying desperately to gain momentum. The shouts, Will screaming my name—it all comes to me as though from a very far distance.

Angus's hair stands out brightly as he closes the distance between us. Almost like a torch rushing at me. The irony isn't lost on me. I exhale, stretching my burning lungs. There's nothing to hide any more—no point. I've made up my mind to do it again. Show what I am.

All his attention is trained on Corbin. The enemy beast.

Angus is almost to me.

I simply let go. My wings surge from my back, ripping through my shirt and cracking on the air.

My wings push free and unfold. Like captive birds the sheets of membrane work on the air, eager to taste sky. Heat explodes in my chest, bursting from my lips in a great ball of red-blue flame. Angus flies backwards from the blast of fire that I'm careful to aim in front of him, barely singeing him.

Tendrils of fire lick up his right arm. He bats at them fiercely, shrieking. One of his comrades hops on him and rolls him on the ground. It takes only a moment for the other hunters to charge me. Now they see me. Their faces twist red with fury as they aim their weapons.

Steam slides from my lips and seeps from my nose, weaving like ribbons into the air. I nod at Angus, flanked by other hunters, silently conveying to them to bring it. I'm ready.

Then Will's there—where he shouldn't be! Standing squarely in front of me. It doesn't stop them though. Not from trying to get to me.

One of the hunters raises the butt end of his rifle, aiming it for Will's face.

'Will!' I scream, my voice lost to draki speech, the sound a deep, inhuman cry. Everyone flinches.

Then my scream is forgotten. I'm forgotten.

A trainlike roar of spinning earth devours everyone, blinding us all. I can't see anything. I hear only a deafening howl as a huge wall of earth surges up in front of the hunters.

Will. He's doing this.

The whirlwind spins all around me, pebbles and twigs striking me everywhere, tearing my flesh. Not about to let Will's efforts go to waste, I drop back down and feel for Corbin, grab him under the shoulders, and haul him into the cover of trees, coughing against the dirt, unsure how long Will can keep this up.

I drag Corbin until my muscles burn from the strain, arms shaking, and then I keep going, the sounds of Will's work a distant groan.

'Cassian!' I scream, hoping he can hear me.

Releasing Corbin, I squat down next to him. I examine the arrow. His pain-glazed eyes focus on me. 'Don't take it out,' I instruct. 'Wait until we get back to the pride.'

'Jacinda,' he chokes, 'I—I'm sorry—'

I shake my head and press fingers to his lips. 'Shut it. You're going to be fine. Don't go making apologies like you're dying. Besides, you probably don't mean it anyway. We both know you're a jerk.'

He starts laughing but ends up in a violent coughing spasm.

I grunt. 'I'll be right back.'

'I'll be here.'

I wince. Of course he will.

I turn back for the river. For Will. For Cassian.

The dirt is everywhere, inescapable, so thick and swirling. Like a sandstorm I can hardly see through. My draki eyes fight to adjust, assessing my surroundings, peering into the chalky brown all around me.

I just need to find Cassian, to reach Will and get him out of here, to locate Tamra so that she can shade the hunters. Then we'll be fine. We'll be free. I cling to this hope, this belief as I stagger back into the fray.

I detect a tall and lean shape in all the swirling brown. 'Will,' I shout, hoping that he can hear me over the roaring wind, even in my unrecognizable draki speech. By now he should know my voice, no matter the language.

The wind alters, grows more alive, more violent. Doesn't he know he can ease up? I fight against the barrage to reach his side. Particles sting my skin like needles. Holding a hand over my face in a weak attempt to protect my eyes, I look up, squinting against the assault of grit.

For a moment, I think I see rippling shadows, dark shapes swirling through the flying earth and debris—like murky forms moving through swamp waters—but with the opaque air it's impossible to tell for sure what's real.

I move towards Will, clenching my teeth as I battle for every step against the powerful wind, my wings folded so they don't catch air and pull me back. I'm almost to him, my aching eyes devouring the sight of him—and then he's gone, down, laid flat on his back by a swooping draki clearly unaware that Will is helping.

Instantly, the tornado of dirt dies, Will's concentration severed. He grabs at his face, and I glimpse blood streaming between his fingers where the draki clawed him.

I blink and scan everything in a glance. Chaos reigns as half a dozen draki screech across the sky, diving at the hunters. They're all onyx, the soldiers of our pride . . . doing what they've been trained all their lives to do. Cassian is there, chasing a hunter into the river, his great leathery wings stretched wide in a low fluid glide.

With a desperate glance at Will, I shout for Cassian, but he doesn't look back. He's full of cold resolve, eager for payback. I feel this. It wraps around me like a hunger.

If Will and I are going to get out of this, we're going to have to do it on our own.

Several draki circle above, carrion birds on the clearing air, calling to one another in guttural cries. Will lies exposed, an easy target. Fear for him coats my mouth as I rush towards him.

I spot Severin, sweeping high over the scene. His wings are large, nicked in spots, the tips jagged and irregular in shape. His gaze sharpens on Will and he screeches.

I dive for Will, determined to shield him.

And that's when Tamra and Deghan emerge side by side from the trees. Fully manifested, they look powerful and magnificent, a daunting pair.

'Tamra,' I shout as I help Will to his feet, wincing at the bloody gashes scoring his face. 'Shade them, Tamra!'

It's the only way to end it—before every last hunter is killed. Maybe I wouldn't have cared before, but now . . . with Miram's and Xander's motionless bodies mere feet away, I just want this to stop before more blood is shed.

I'm sick of it all. And these are Will's family and friends. I don't want their deaths on his conscience, and I know it would weigh on him. On us both.

Tamra nods purposefully and steps forward. Amid the gunfire, shouts, and screeching draki, she holds out her arms and mist begins to flow.

Standing close to Will, I watch, marvelling at my sister's gift. She possesses a talent that can save lives. As a shader, she is hope and salvation.

The mist doesn't have a chance to build and rise. One of the many bullets zooming through the air finds its mark.

I scream as Tamra staggers from the impact, one hand flying to her head where blood pours. She lowers her hand, stares at it with incomprehension.

My agony is intense . . . the closest thing I ever felt before was losing Dad.

Deghan grabs hold of Tamra. Her head lolls and then sags against his shoulder. He lowers her to the ground, shouting her name. The anguish in his expression echoes what spins inside me.

Almost immediately, the shielding fog begins to evaporate, and we're exposed again, caught back in a war zone with nowhere to hide.

'Tamra!' I scream. I move towards her, one arm still wrapped around Will's waist, unwilling to let him go.

It's slow going, and I think I'll never reach her when my back explodes in pain, propelling me forward.

I land chest first on the ground, unable to move, too stunned, too hurt. My vision grows fuzzy, tear-blurred. I try to speak, cry out. Pain radiates up and down the length of my body. Even so, the physical aches are no competition for the misery of my heart. *Tamra. Tamra!*

Will's face is there, filling my vision. His mouth forms my name. He touches my face, but oddly everything is silent around me, like someone stuffed cotton in my ears.

I feel my lips part, speak, say something. I can't be sure what—not while I can't hear my own voice. Not while a million thoughts ricochet through me.

I think I say Will's name. Tamra. Mum.

Help, help, help . . .

Then nothing as darkness rolls in.

CHAPTER TWENTY-THREE

Snatches of light drift in and out, fracturing the dark, offering hope one second and then bleak nothingness the next. Voices rumble past like distant thunder, so close I can almost understand, almost make out the words.

But it's impossible to concentrate when all my world is pain.

'She's not going to make it . . .'

'Don't say that. Never say that.' Wincing, I turn towards the sound of this voice, knowing it on an instinctive level even when I can't arrive at the name. Can't form it in my head. Because I can't *think* . . . only feel.

Then, like the fading of a morning mist, the voices die away. Everything vanishes. Including me.

* * *

Pain brings me back. Every time I open my eyes it's to this anguish, blinding me to all else. It's the only thing that convinces me I'm still alive.

Faces flash. Hands hold me down. None of it registers. None of it sinks into me like the burning torment of my body. The agony radiates through all of me. The heat . . . even the heat is too much for me.

The only thing I can do is surrender to the blanket of dark where I feel nothing, see nothing. Where even nightmares cannot find me. No pride. No hunters. Nothing.

Where I can cease to exist.

Whispers become louder in my ears—grow into real, actual voices. Words and not slivers of dreams. They coax me back to the living. Become more than ghostly sounds that overlap in my head.

I recognize them. Nidia. Tamra.

Tamra! She's alive. Like a balm to my wounds, this knowledge fortifies me.

And there's another voice I more than recognize. A voice I know deep in every pore, in my soul—Will's.

'Will,' I rasp, trying to lift my head, questions buzzing through me.

I hear the smile in his voice, the joy. 'Welcome back, Jacinda.'

I blink slowly, opening my eyes to a shadowy world.

Blurry faces are there, but before I can focus on them I have to close my eyes against the sudden dizziness that assaults me.

I open my mouth and shut it again at the scratchy dryness. A cup is pressed upon me and I drink greedily, ignoring the tart tang of verda root lacing the water. As the cup leaves my lips, I turn my head. A cool touch brushes my cheek, and it's only then that I realize I'm lying flat on my stomach, my left cheek against the cool sheet of a mattress.

I reopen my eyes again and find the world is no longer spinning. 'Hunters . . . Tamra . . . ,' I get out, the fear still there, a fresh wound. For me, it was only moments ago that I fought for my life, the life of my sister and friends . . . Will . . .

Tamra's voice comes to me again. More than a whisper this time. 'I'm OK, Jacinda. The bullet just grazed me. Bled a lot, but nothing more. Nidia patched me up.'

'The hunters are gone,' Nidia's voice reassures me. 'We moved them miles away. They'll have no memory of what happened. I saw to that.'

Relief eases through me. I fight to clear the last of the fuzziness from my vision, and when I do, it's to see the person I've been longing for. *Will.*

I just manage to sigh his name before Nidia's drink takes hold of me and drags me back under.

'Jacinda, you have visitors.' The voice pulls me from my light doze. I open my eyes and slowly turn my head.

I'd fallen back asleep shortly after my reunion with Will and Tamra. After Nidia forced some broth down me. Once I had been assured that Will, Tamra, Cassian, and Deghan were all safe, it had been a relief to sink back into sleep without any lurking worry. Except for Miram, we all made it. And at the moment no one in the pride seemed intent on destroying Will. Double bonus. I could sleep free of fear . . . I'm not sure when I last felt that way.

I'd rolled onto my back. The pressure wasn't too terrible and it felt good to shift positions. I glance at Will in a chair to my right and Nidia standing over me. I nod at her as I manoeuvre myself carefully into a sitting position, mindful of my still-tender back. Nidia quickly rearranges the pillows behind me.

'Are you up to it?' Will asks, setting down the book he's been reading on the bed.

I nod, even though I'm unsure what *it* is.

Footsteps march across Nidia's floors outside the bedroom. I run fingers through my matted hair, wishing for a mirror and then deciding it's best that I don't know what I look like.

As the elders clear the threshold one by one, I hold my breath, expecting to see Severin, but he never enters the room. And then I guess that shouldn't be so surprising, after all. He just learned his daughter died . . . at the hands of his sister. Even if he wanted to continue on in his role as alpha, I'm not sure he could. Even if he was emotionally capable of it, the crimes of his sister would no doubt overshadow him.

The last to step inside is Cassian, and my suspicions are confirmed. If Cassian is here, he must have taken Severin's place.

My breath catches. He's undoubtedly proven himself. He will make a much better leader. And it explains why Will is unharmed. My gaze roves over Cassian's tall form. He looks healed. No sign of injuries. The last time I saw him he was busy killing hunters as fast as he could. To avenge Miram. I feel a pang in my chest at the thought of her murder. I play with the edge of the sheet, wanting to say something . . . stretch out a hand and touch him, ease the answering pain that reaches me through our bond, threatening to consume me. His expression reveals nothing, but he can't hide his grief. Not from me.

'Jacinda, we've come to ask for your accounting.'

My gaze darts between Will and Cassian. 'You haven't heard it all yet?'

The elder who spoke inclines his head. 'We have received reports on Miram's death from your sister, the draki who calls himself Deghan, and Corbin. But we need to hear from you.' Corbin? Did he speak the truth? I assess each of the elders' faces, trying to gauge their thoughts.

'I witnessed Jabel kill Miram and then throw her in the river.' I moisten my lips and glance at Cassian, hating to say words that I know must pain him. But not saying them won't make it less true. Sucking in a breath, I add, 'She did it without blinking an eye.'

A muscle flickers in Cassian's cheek. Otherwise, he shows no outward sign that my words affect him. He gives no hint as to the rage and grief that surge inside him. But I feel it. My breath escapes in a hiss between my teeth and I clench my hand in the sheets as I battle the onslaught of emotions.

'I don't think she's up to this,' Nidia interjects, sending a reproving look at all the elders, lingering on Cassian the longest. She knows what's really bothering me—that Cassian's emotions are crippling me.

'She said the same thing we all did,' Will comments.

'Even Corbin,' Nidia says pointedly, surprising me. Corbin told the truth? If Jabel's own son implicated her, they have no reason to doubt our version of events. Not with Corbin corroborating it.

'We have what we wanted. Let's leave her. She needs her rest,' Cassian announces.

Everyone files from the room except Cassian. He hesitates, adjusting his weight from foot to foot. 'I'm glad you're all right.' I notice his hands shut into fists at his sides. 'I should have been there for you.' His gaze slides to Will, and I know he's thinking that Will was there. He gives him a slight nod, acknowledging this.

'You don't owe me an apology.'

'Yeah, well, I'm glad Will and Tamra were with you.'

'That was the plan when we agreed for you to go into the pride. We would stay behind and wait. I knew the risks coming back here. None of us—' I stop abruptly just before saying no one got hurt. We lost Miram. My eyes sting at the reminder. It shouldn't have happened but it did. 'I'm so sorry about Miram, Cassian.'

The vertical pupils vibrate with the magnitude of his pain. 'I shouldn't have left her—'

'No, I should have protected her better. You left her with me—'

He shakes his head. 'She was my responsibility. I failed her.'

'Your own aunt killed her.' Nidia's voice is soothing and firm at the same time. 'Just as we're all sure she is the one who betrayed Magnus. There's not much you can do when you're in bed with a serpent and don't know it.'

Cassian nods, but I know he's unconvinced. He'll forever suffer guilt for his sister's death.

He inches toward the door. 'I'll come by later.'

Part of me wants to ask him to stay, but then I'll have to endure all his emotions, terrible as they are right now. Selfish or not, I'd rather he go.

I smile tentatively as his gaze sweeps over me propped up in the bed. And in that look, I know he senses my hope. For me, for himself, he'll stay away.

Will looks nervous as we take the first step outside Nidia's cottage into the swirl of mist.

'Stop looking so worried,' I say, bumping him lightly with my hip. Not too strongly. I wouldn't want to lose my balance and fall over.

'Seeing as you only just woke up today and can barely walk, I'm the one who's going to get into trouble if we get caught.'

'Then hurry before Nidia notices I'm missing.'

One arm around my waist, Will takes the bulk of my weight and guides me through the township, following my directions north through the town centre and then west, past houses towards the burial grounds.

I inhale deeply the night's cool, loamy air, letting it feed my spirit. I feel the burial grounds before they come into sight. The songs of the dead reach me through the stones that bear their imprint. We pass through a screen of pines until we reach the clearing . . . where all draki are laid to rest. Gems of every variety cover the ground—some on the surface and some buried, nestled deep in the earth and ashes of draki long since passed. They glow, colouring the night, suffusing the air in a rainbow of muted shades.

Will gasps beside me.

'It's beautiful, isn't it?' I murmur.

'I—I . . . ,' he stammers.

'You feel them,' I supply.

He blinks several times, overcome. A feeling I understand. They're here. All of them. *Miram, too.* The memory of every draki, whether I knew them or not, lingers here. Their energy crackles on the air and reaches deep inside me.

'Dad needs to be here,' I say. 'Tam and I will have to pick a stone . . . leave it for him.' It's hard uttering these words. Without proof of his death, without his ashes, we'd never considered doing such a thing before. But the time has come.

Will nods in agreement, his expression solemn. 'You should do that.'

The gems wink from their earthen beds. One in particular catches my gaze. A topaz. Miram's gemstone. I breathe her name. There are several topazes in the graveyard of ash and jewels . . . but this one speaks to me, calls to me as if it were Miram herself. And I can't help thinking it might be.

I blink burning eyes. My legs suddenly give out and Will catches me, swings me up in his arms.

'I'm sorry.' I weep into his shoulder, loathing that I should be so weak. After everything, shouldn't I be tougher than this? Immune to such loss?

'Don't apologize.' He eases us down, holding me like a child in his arms and crooning nonsense in my ear. His hand is strong and firm at my back. His touch moves to my head, strokes my hair. 'She deserves to be remembered . . . and missed.'

I hiccup through my tears. 'We set out to save her . . . and she ended up dead anyway.' The reality of it only makes the grief that much more bitter. 'One of us murdered her . . . not the enkros or hunters. A draki. Her own aunt killed her. And my dad.'

I beat my fist on the ground, striking a gemstone, the edge of which cuts my hand. I hiss. Shimmering blood, almost black in the night, the purple hue undetectable, wells up on my skin. Will mutters a curse and uses his shirt to dab it clean.

'Hey, be careful. You're injured enough,' he chides, pulling my head down to his shoulder, and I spend myself, crying not over the pain in my hand but the pain in my heart.

'I've soaked your shirt,' I point out, plucking at the wet fabric stretching over his shoulder.

'And bloodied it,' he mock accuses.

I sniff and smile, smoothing a hand over his shoulder. We're quiet for some moments, sitting together in the gem light.

'What'd they do to her?' I ask, and clarify, in case he mistakes my meaning, 'Jabel.'

He sighs. 'There was to be a trial . . .'

'Was?'

'According to Nidia, she knew what the outcome would be.'

My heart thumps faster. 'The sentence would be death.' For what she did . . . pride justice would be swift and merciless. 'Nothing less than she deserved for gutting her own niece like she was garbage to be discarded.' I shake my head, aware that I sound hard, but on this matter I don't care. 'I'll never forget the image of Miram being flung into that water.'

Will holds me closer. 'Jabel escaped before they could—'

'She got away then,' I state, the words hard as I think about her. Out there. Unpunished. For Miram. For Dad.

'She'll hardly be happy, Jacinda. All alone among humans. She's not you. She killed to protect this life.' He motions around us. 'Now she's lost it.'

It's not enough. 'Forgive me if I fail to feel satisfied. I still think execution would be better.'

'You're going to have to let it go.' He brushes the hair back from my cheek. 'Don't you think there's been enough bloodshed?' The sentiment echoes my own not that long ago, and I fall quiet, pensive, unable to argue the point.

Will reaches for my hand and laces our fingers so that I feel the thud of his pulse. His hazel eyes search mine, trying to see inside me. Almost like he's concerned I've come out of all this damaged . . . or maybe just the girl I used to be. A girl who's on a mission to save everyone— without room enough in her life for him because she's busy seeking justice that's not always there to be had.

I cover our linked hands with my free one and lean forward, hungry to reach him, touch him—be as close as I can get. And leave the old Jacinda behind.

CHAPTER TWENTY-FOUR

It's a rare sunny day as I walk through the township with Tamra's arm wrapped around my waist. A slight mist that has managed to survive the greedy rays floats above our heads, thin enough for the sunlight to filter down and warm my hair.

It's my first sanctioned outing since I woke, since Cassian and the elders visited me three days ago. Before that, I was unconscious for four days. Unbeknownst to me, in that week, my world was reborn.

'It feels different,' I say as two girls rush past us towards school. Late, presumably.

'Since Severin stepped down, it is different.'

Remy walks by and nods hello. I notice his patrol armband is gone.

'No armband,' I murmur.

'They got rid of them.' The armbands represented a divided pride to me. Those who wore them had been the enforcers, the rest of us the subjugated.

'Can't say I miss the sight of them.' I nod in satisfaction, knowing who was behind the order. 'Cassian will do good things for the pride,' I add.

Tamra gives me a funny look but says nothing.

A group appears in the distance, seven or eight draki returning with the fresh catch of the day. I blink when I recognize two among them.

'Will? Deghan?'

They break from the group when they see us. Grinning, they hold up their stringers of fish. Deghan ducks low to kiss Tamra, right there in the middle of the township, in broad daylight. I try not to stare but it's not a common sight. And it's no *little* kiss. It's the kiss a man gives to a woman when he's freed from prison.

I can't help but smile because I guess that's an apt description for Deghan. They're still kissing when I look at Will.

And then I forget about them.

I never could see much else when he was around. I look into his changeable eyes . . . right now they're a goldish brown. His hair falls down his forehead. It needs cutting. Or maybe not. There's just more for me to touch, more to slide my fingers through.

He lowers his head and gives me a slow, easy kiss, his lips smooth and cool as the mountain air. 'Hi,' he says in that velvet voice that sends shivers through me.

'Hi,' I return, gesturing to the fish. 'Nice catch.'

'Yeah. I'm kind of impressed with myself. I always thought redheads were sexy.'

'Ha-ha. I meant the fish.'

'Ah. Yes.' He pulls back to lift his stringer aloft and

admire his haul before looking back at me. 'How are you feeling today?'

'Good. Nice to see you earning your keep around here,' I tease.

'Nice to know I can . . . and not, you know, be—'

'Killed,' I finish.

He nods. And the strangeness of this isn't lost on me. Will. In the pride. Doing ordinary things. Belonging.

'C'mon, Will. Let's go clean these,' Deghan says.

Will nods, still holding my gaze. 'I'll come by later tonight.'

'Great, but you smell like fish. Clean up first.'

His smile broadens, and I feel light, buoyant just to see him happy here. *Here.* A prospect I always hoped could happen but never really imagined possible.

Tamra and I move on, both revelling in the aftermath of moments with boys we love. Who would have ever thought this would become our reality? Even now it feels like a dream . . . something that might be snatched away at any moment.

We stop at the small playground outside the primary school. A dozen children play, zipping down the slide or climbing the rock wall. The teacher supervising smiles and waves at us. I wave back awkwardly. It feels weird to be accepted again.

Two girls race to the last available swing. The one who reaches it first hops on with a triumphant smile. The other girl sticks out her tongue and sashays off like she has something better to do.

I grin. 'Remember when we were like that?'

Az comes out of the classroom door right then, and I remember that she works as a teacher's aide for her duty.

She stopped by to see me yesterday, fussing over me for getting caught by hunters again, and then catching me up on all the pride gossip.

She runs to the edge of the playground when she sees us, her long hair a black banner streaked with blue. 'Hey, good to see you walking around. Tired of bed?' She hugs me. 'I mean how boring must it be having a gorgeous guy waiting on you at your bedside?' She rolls her eyes.

'And you?' She points a finger at Tamra. 'Better keep that Deghan of yours close. Have you seen all the girls staring after him?' She presses a hand to her chest. 'Not me, of course.' She winks at me. 'I have more respect than to drool over another girl's guy.'

'Az!' The teacher calls out from across the playground.

'Gotta run.' Az sighs. 'Some of us have duties . . . you know, instead of adventures with hot boys.'

Tamra and I are chuckling as she darts away.

'Oh, I've missed her,' I say, shaking my head. Turning, I examine Tamra's profile thoughtfully. 'I'm going to miss you, too.'

Tamra's features turn wistful. 'You can stay here now, you know. Will, too.' She bites her lip, releasing it to say, almost as though she's reading my thoughts, 'It will be different now.'

'I know that.'

'And it's not as though Will is quite human either.'

I nod. That's true. I draw a deep breath and consider Will. The verdict's still out on him. He's not a draki but not human either. He has powers, true . . . but did the draki blood extend his life, too? Only time will tell.

'I know the pride is a better place now. With Cassian—'

'Jacinda.'

Something in Tam's voice stops me. Her arm slips from around my waist. I turn to face her, gingerly positioning myself before her.

'What if Cassian weren't in charge?'

My eyebrows furrow 'Who else . . .'

'Last night Cassian and the remaining elders came to see me.'

I tip my head to the side, waiting for her to explain.

'They don't want one alpha at the helm anymore. They want to keep it a council made up of representatives . . .'

She flounders for a moment.

She looks out at the playing children, and I can't help wondering who among them might be a fire-breather, or a defunct draki like everyone thought Tamra was. And whether the new pride will treat them both with fairness.

A breeze whips fiery tendrils across my face and I scrape them back. 'Well. That sounds very democratic.'

She finally continues. 'They want me to be on the council. And Deghan.'

I pull back. Angling my head, I look at her, marvelling that my sister has become someone others admire. I've always known there was greatness in her, but until recently the pride never realized it. 'And I can hear in your voice that you're interested.'

'I said yes.'

'I see.' Nodding slowly, I process this and tell myself I should have been prepared for this. She had already told me as much . . . that she wanted to remain with the pride. It's not really a shock. Since Deghan, things have changed. Tamra would no longer be content to follow me through life. A good thing, I know. We'll be sisters, always, and still love each other, just lead separate lives. That's as it should be. Still . . . it's an adjustment thinking of my future without her next to me. And it stings a little. 'You'll be good for the pride. Fair. They're lucky to have you.' The words are tight in my throat, but I manage to get them out.

If I told her about Mum would she still want to remain here? Even as I wonder, I know it's not fair to manipulate her with that information just because I don't want to lose her. But then can I *not* tell her? It's not something I can keep to myself

'We're not little girls any more,' she murmurs.

'No. We're not,' I agree. A silence falls. 'I know where to find Mum,' I finally admit. 'Remember our trip to Oregon? That picture of us in front of the rock formation that looked like a palm tree?'

Tamra nods, her expression brightening. 'Yes! The palm tree!'

'She's there,' I say. 'She's gone back there.' I watch Tamra, hoping—unfairly, I know—that this might change her mind.

Instead, she says, 'Well, she can come back here now. Her banishment won't stand any more—'

'I doubt she'll care.' I give Tamra a look. 'You don't expect her to want to live here again, do you? She's never wanted that.'

Tamra sighs. 'You're right.'

And then I feel bad . . . for trying to use Mum against her. 'I'm sure she'll visit,' I say. 'She'll be glad you're happy. I am, too.'

She looks at me with relief.

I shake my head, thinking of something else. 'What about Cassian? Is he content just being another member of this council?'

She looks at me like I should already know this answer. 'He's leaving.'

'What?'

'He's leaving the pride.'

Suddenly it's hard to breathe.

She stares at me in concern. 'Jacinda? Are you OK?'

'The pride needs him.' That's what he always told me—that the pride needed him. *Us*. He'd almost convinced me of that.

'He doesn't seem to think so any more. His dad stepped down. Severin is broken, ashamed. Him and Corbin both.' She moistens her lips and stares back out at the children. 'I don't think Cassian can stay here any more. Not after everything that's happened.'

And I guess I understand that. I don't see him remaining here, fading, disappearing into shadow alongside his father and cousin. Not that I'm lumping him in with Severin and Corbin. They're struggling with their shame while he battles with his grief for Miram. My eyes close in a pained blink as Miram's face swims before me. I know him well enough to know he's blaming himself. 'I guess that's true.'

'What about you, Jacinda? What are you going to do?'

What am I going to do? It's the question I've been asking myself for months now. Even longer than that. Even before there was Will tugging me one way and Cassian another . . .

When it all comes down to me—-just me—what do *I* want? Where am I supposed to be? For the first time, I have the freedom to make that choice. A slow smile takes over my lips.

I loop my arm through Tamra's and we move away from the playground. The children's laughter fades behind us. 'Believe it or not, I'm still figuring that out. First, of course, Will and I are going to find Mum. And then . . . ' My voice dies away and I feel my smile stretch wider.

She nudges me playfully. 'What are you smiling about?'

'Nothing. Just feels good to have a choice. Until now, I've never really had the freedom to decide and then make that decision a reality. But wherever I go, I'll come back to visit. I have to see my hotshot sister leading the pride into the future, after all.'

Tamra rolls her eyes.

'Now, c'mon,' I say. 'All this walking has made me famished.'

CHAPTER TWENTY-FIVE

I tiptoe down the darkened hallway of Nidia's house, taking special care as I enter the living room where Will sleeps on the couch. I watch him for a moment, appreciating the rugged beauty of him before slipping outside. I need to do this alone. No sense waking him.

The township hums with all the sounds of night, but no one else is about as I move north toward Cassian's house. A light flows through the shades. Someone's up. I think of Severin. Tamra called him ashamed. Broken. It's hard summoning remorse for the man. I know he lost his daughter . . . and, in a manner, his sister, too.

Squaring my shoulders, I knock and wait, hoping Severin doesn't open the door. I know Jabel was responsible for my father's death and not him, but he still played his part in my life's miseries. I don't want to look on his face again if I don't have to.

I know who's on the other side of the door before it opens. I feel him as keenly as my own breath spilling from my lips.

'Jacinda.' His gaze sweeps over me in my nightgown and then looks over my shoulder. 'You came alone?'

I nod.

He gestures behind him. 'Come in.'

I wave to the porch swing. 'Can we sit out here?'

He closes the door behind him and takes a seat. I sit beside him. For a while, we just swing, and I wonder if this is how it would have been if I had never left the pride. Cassian and I rocking together on porch swings in the evenings for the rest of our lives?

'You're leaving,' I announce.

He inclines his head. 'Yes. So are you.' Not a question.

'Yes. Where will you go?'

He flips a hand idly through the air. 'I don't know. There's a lot to see out there . . . other prides. I'd like to connect with them. Share what I've learned, warn them about the enkros and their tracking devices. Maybe I'll learn from them, too.'

I think of Lia, Roc, and the others—wonder if they made it. A bitter taste coats my mouth.

'I'm sure there are better places for me than here,' he adds.

I turn to him. 'What are you looking for?'

'Maybe somewhere that I can contribute something good.'

'You can do that here.'

He winces. One corner of his mouth curls in a partial smile. 'Then maybe somewhere I can forget. How's that for honesty?'

His purply dark eyes cut into me, and I know he's talking about more than his family, more than his sister.

I open my mouth, but he holds up a hand to stop me. 'I get it, Jacinda. I didn't before, but now . . . since we were bonded.' He laughs harshly, and there's discomfort in the sound. 'I understand what it is you feel for Will. God, do I understand.'

My cheeks heat with embarrassment, the meaning behind his words sinking in. While I felt everything Cassian felt, he's been experiencing all my feelings, too. Even my feelings for Will.

'Wow,' I murmur. 'This is kind of awkward.'

He laughs again and this time the sound is genuine.

I brush a strand of hair from my face, but it falls back over my eyes. Our gazes lock. 'I hope you find what you're searching for out there.' *What you deserve.*

He lifts a hand and tucks the errant hair behind my ear. 'You, too, Jacinda.'

Without another word, he drops his hand and moves toward the door. There he pauses and looks back at me. 'Goodbye, Jacinda.'

I drag a deep shuddery breath into my lungs, knowing that I may not see him again—ever. 'Goodbye, Cassian.'

Then, he's gone. The door clicks softly behind him.

I rise, unable to stay another moment on his front porch, in such close proximity that I can feel his every emotion. None of which are pleasant at this particular time. Sorrow. Grief. A weariness that runs soul deep.

But what I don't sense from him is regret. This is what I take with me as I flee his porch. What I cling to. The knowledge that we're both following our hearts without regret. And right now mine is leading me to Will.

I hurry down the path, my nightgown swishing at my ankles. Suddenly a figure emerges from the mist.

I gasp and step back until I see that it's Will. 'You scared me.'

He approaches slowly, hands buried deep in his jeans pockets.

'Sorry. I woke up as you were leaving. I was worried about you.' I can't imagine what he thought . . . me sneaking out in the middle of the night and going to Cassian of all people. Still, I see no anger in his face. Only patience. He's watching me, waiting it seems, his gaze not so much wary as guarded. I've led him to hell and back, but he's been there with me through it all.

'I'm fine. Cassian and I were just saying goodbye.' I look back over my shoulder. 'He won't be here in the morning.' I know this without being told directly. I feel it. He'd been waiting for me to come. Waiting to say his final goodbye.

Will looks over my shoulder, peering at Cassian's quiet house. A breeze stirs, and the swing rocks on the porch. 'He's going?'

'Yes.' I take Will's hand. His long fingers wrap around mine. 'He'll be OK,' I say, believing it. Cassian will find what he needs. Elsewhere.

I start to walk, but Will makes me stop and face him. 'Are *you* OK?' His brow creases with concern.

I lean forward and smooth out the lines on his forehead before sliding both my hands along his cheeks, holding his face tenderly between my palms. 'It's finally done. We're free.' At last. 'We can go anywhere.' I press my mouth to his, kiss him with everything, all that I am—until that familiar heat builds up in my core and I feel ready to burst from my skin. I pull back and say huskily against his lips, 'I'm more than OK.'

He hauls me back and kisses me and I don't need a bond to sense if he's OK.

I know he is. We both are.

The ocean is a gentle rush in my ears as I walk hand in hand with Will. In my other hand, the straps of my sandals dangle from my fingers. The rolled hems of my jeans chafe the back of my knees.

'You sure this is it?'

I hold my arm up over my face, shoes swinging. The setting sun paints the air a magnificent pink-orange, so bright it hurts my eyes. Several rock structures dot the coastline. For a moment, I see myself here years ago, running with my sister, Dad and Mum following at a slower pace, holding hands and enjoying watching us as we dart into the rolling surf. Tamra loses a flip-flop and shrieks, splashing into the ocean to retrieve it.

I grin at the memory and let it warm me. 'Yes. I'm sure.'

Will squeezes my hand.

We continue on, my feet sinking into the sand. I walk a steady line even with the dense sand pulling at me. Anticipation trips through me as I scan the shoreline, hoping she's here. That I'm not wrong. I've waited a long time for this. If she isn't here, I'll just keep looking until I find her.

In the meantime Will and I have each other. And all the time in the world for moments like this—the two of us walking together on a beach. Without fear of tomorrow. Without any question of who we are or what we want.

I spot a woman ahead on the beach, her hair partially covered with a purple bandana. The wavy ends lift on the wind like dancing flames as she stares out at the sea. She hugs herself as she gazes resolutely ahead, searching for something in those gold-cast waters and descending sun.

I stop beneath the shadow of one of the rock formations and follow her gaze, staring at the sun sinking into the ocean. My chest tightens. It's a beautiful sight.

'There she is.' Will squeezes my arm. 'Come on.'

I nod, watching her another moment, almost afraid to call out, afraid she might disappear like in my dreams. 'Mum!'

She turns to face me with a suddenness that tells me she's been waiting for me. She knew I would come.

I lace my fingers with Will's. Our palms press flush against each other and I can feel the beat of his heart thumping in rhythm with mine.

'Let's go,' I declare, stepping out from the shadows and into the light.

ACKNOWLEDGEMENTS

After three years buried deep in the world of Firelight, it's hard to say goodbye to Jacinda and friends. But, as in life, all things must come to an end, and I simply consider myself lucky to have been able to share the world of Firelight with so many readers. Thank you for taking the journey with me.

I want to give a special thanks to everyone at HarperCollins for getting behind this series. Of course, none of it could have happened without my wonderful editors, Farrin Jacobs and Kari Sutherland. Farrin, thank you for taking a look at a "dragon story" in the first place and giving it (and me!) a chance. Your support has meant so much. Kari, your eye for detail never ceases to amaze. Thanks for never settling for "good enough". The end results are as much yours as mine.

A big hug goes to my agent, Maura Kye-Casella, for being in my corner all these years. We've come far together. I've never doubted our partnership and count my lucky stars that I signed with you right out of the gate. Publicist extraordinaire, Marisa Russell, thanks for being on top of everything and always working so quickly—especially when I slam you with emails. Sasha Illingworth, Cara Petrus, and Sarah Kaufman—thanks for creating such marvellous covers. Tera Lynn Childs, you were the first one to tell me to go for it—thank you.

I'm lucky to be surrounded with family and friends whose support helps keep me afloat: Tera Lynn Childs (again!), Sarah MacLean, Jane Welborn, Lindsay Marsh, Mary Lindsey, Shana Galen, Vicky Dreiling, Kerrelyn Sparks, Kady Cross, Kim Lenox, Ginny Endecott, and Laura Griffin. And to my parents, Gene and Marilyn Michels, thanks for always being proud of me—and bragging to anyone who will listen. Robert Michels and Rosanne Kohler, you're guilty of the same—love and thanks to you both.

And for my children, who keep everything in perspective, you add joy and meaning to every day. I'm a better writer for it. And finally—Jared. With each day that passes, I value and appreciate you more than the day before. You make everything possible. I love you. I love our life.

ABOUT THE AUTHOR

SOPHIE JORDAN grew up on a pecan farm in the Texas Hill Country, where she wove fantasies of dragons, warriors, and princesses. A former high school English teacher, she's also the *New York Times* bestselling author of historical romances. She now lives in Houston with her family. When she's not writing, she spends her time overloading on caffeine (lattes and Diet cherry Coke preferred) and talking plotlines with anyone who will listen (including her kids), and cramming her DVR with true-crime and reality-TV shows. Sophie also writes paranormal romances under the name Sharie Kohler. You can visit her online at *www.sophiejordan.net*.

Every moment with Will, I feel at risk, exposed. Danger hangs close, as tangible as the heavy mists I've left behind. And I can't get enough of it. Of him.

When Jacinda meets Will, she knows she should avoid him at all costs. She is a Draki—a descendant of dragons with the power to shift into human form. He is a draki hunter, who could destroy her if he ever finds out the truth.

But Jacinda can't resist getting closer to him. Even if it means risking the draki's most closely guarded secret—and her life.

9780192756510

I remember Will's promise:
'It's not over. I'll find you . . .'
Then it dawns on me. He'll just think I left. Vanished.

Jacinda did the unthinkable for love: she betrayed the most closely-
guarded secret of her kind.

Exposed for what she really is—a descendant of dragons with the
ability to shift into human form—she must return to her pride
knowing she might never see Will again.

Jacinda knows she should just forget him, yet she clings to the hope
that they'll be together again. So when the chance arrives to follow
her heart, will she risk everything?

9780192756541